Valentine's Heart

By Merri Bright

Valentine's Heart

The Billionaire's Betasitter

Merri Bright

Editing by Aubergine Editing

Cover by Y'all That Graphic

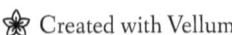 Created with Vellum

For Mr. Bright, who is my favorite Valentine.

Contents

Content Advisory 1

1. Valentine 3

2. Donovan 13

3. Valentine 20

4. Donovan 25

5. Valentine 32

6. Valentine 39

7. Donovan 45

8. Valentine 53

9. Donovan 68

10. Valentine 79

11. Donovan 84

12. Valentine 92

13. Donovan 98

14. Valentine 102

15. Donovan 105

16. Valentine 110

Epilogue 119

Acknowledgments 125

Also by Merri Bright 127

About the Author 129

Content Advisory

Welcome to The Billionaire's Betasitter series! If you love to laugh while you read, and you're not afraid of spicy stories, dig in. If you are easily offended by on-page sexytimes, profanity, or age-gap storylines, put this book down and back away.

This novella is chock full of *knottiness*. The characters in this human Omegaverse romance are called betas (normal humans), omegas (typically women with soothing pheromones and ramped-up sex drives), and alphas (men and a few women who are assertive, respected, and attracted to omegas). Omegas and alphas together make up around ten percent of the population. In this world, fated mates called "true mates" exist, but are not that easy to find.

This "one-sausage special" has a lot of spicy ingredients, including, but not limited to: unique identifying scents, heat cycles for the omegas, unusual peen, breeding, knotting, dirty talk/praise, claiming, backdoor action, fun with toys, and the use of the terms Daddy and baby girl.

1

It also touches on past sexual trauma of both MCs as teens, mental health issues/ panic disorder, and a mention of past child abduction (FMC). Please take care of yourself when choosing to read.

Chapter 1

Valentine

The Mile High Club in Aspen smelled like fryer oil, cheap beer, tequila, and pumped-in chemical deodorizer. In other words, what most twenty-one-year-old women would call a good time.

I already regretted coming, and I hadn't even stepped one foot inside.

The stench rushed out the door on a warm gust of air every time someone passed us on their way in or out. Next to me, Victoria, one of my triplet sisters—and the current bane of my existence, since this particular club was her idea—sucked in a deep breath. "Ah, I can smell my next lover already."

I smiled, trying to hide my nerves. "Does it smell like alphas?"

Tori sniffed again, like she was sampling the aroma of a fine wine. "Mmmm. Like future bad decisions and enough liquid courage to make them again and again."

"There may be a few alphas, Val, but this club is a buffet of betas." On my other side, Vanessa unbuttoned her poofy white ski coat, then fluffed the platinum blonde wig she was wearing to hide the brown hair underneath. "Which is why we're here, Tori. Not for you to broaden your alpha palate. Tonight, we need hot, sweaty beta wieners for our sweet, innocent sister to cut her teeth on."

"Teeth?" I blinked. Unlike my amazing, extroverted sisters, I had no idea what men liked. But even I had heard that teeth weren't... *optimal* blow job tools.

Tori snorted. "Don't listen to her, Val. No man wants teeth on their *sausage*. Not even a beta."

Nessa smirked. "I beg to differ. Titchy Meyerson likes it when I use my teeth a little bit."

Faking a dizzy spell, Tori grabbed me with one hand and gasped dramatically at Nessa. "You put Titchy's dick in your mouth? Titchy 'No-Shower November' Meyerson? He did a month of videos on his YouTube channel showing the growth of his neck rings! The man has ablutophobia!"

"He showered for *me*," Nessa said with a casual shrug. "And drank pineapple juice every day the week we were hanging out. Sweetest tadpoles I ever tasted."

"I think I'm g-going to throw up," I told her, not kidding. "I'm g-g-going home."

"Back to the hotel?" Nessa laced her arm through mine.

I thought of my room at our shared apartment in Denver, the piles of fabric waiting to be quilted, the new floor loom in one corner, the recipe book I'd been writing in secret. "No. *Home.*"

Tori scowled. "It's four hours or more in this snow."

Nessa tightened her grip on me. "Not this time. You're going in there, and you're going to find a safe, young beta. A short, sweet guy with small... *feet.*"

"A starter sausage," Tori added. "We made a plan, remember?"

"You can do the plan. I'm n-not sure this w-was such a g-g-great idea." I stopped speaking and closed my eyes for a moment, reminding myself to slow down. Tori waited patiently, understanding what I was doing.

The stutter that I'd conquered years before had returned with a vengeance after I'd spoken to my doctor in late December. Even with all my family around for the holidays, I'd been more than anxious about what was happening to me, physically.

I breathed in for a count of four, out for a count of eight once, then again, remembering the techniques I'd been using since I was a young girl. I knew how to control my stutter. I'd been through a decade and a half of the most expensive speech therapy money could buy; in fact, I suspected I was personally responsible for my speech therapist putting her kid through college. I'd practiced meditation and mindfulness. I *knew* how to keep control of my voice, and my mind, and my emotions.

And no one else knew we were here, so our evening should be easy. Safe. Like normal young women got to experience all the time, without wondering if they were being watched by paparazzi.

Without feeling like time was running out.

Time *was* running out, though. I knew that. It was my doctor who'd helped me and my sisters come up with this plan. A safe way for me to step into the next phase of my life. Adulthood. Sexual maturity.

Sheer freaking terror.

Nessa leaned down. "You know you're just going in to check out the guys. You never have to do anything you don't want."

Tori nodded. "We've gone over all the 'emergency exits' if your hookup does anything shady." She held up her phone.

"Just text V to either one of us, or flash two fingers. You'll get emergency texts from both of us. Be prepared to fake cry."

"Or to say your ex-boyfriend just escaped federal prison and is on his way. Mutter something about Chainsaw Charlie."

I almost cracked a smile.

Tori frowned. "Worst case, you could always say you have explosive diarrhea. That'd work if anyone creepy gets handsy in the club, too."

"No, no, in the club, all she has to do is fake choke," Nessa argued. "Val, you can be 'allergic' to something in the drink, or the bar mix, and start choking like you're anaphylactic. They put Brazil nuts in sometimes—"

"Or you could overshare!" Tori broke in. "Tell them about your first kiss, or your first boyfr—" She stopped. They knew as well as I did, there was nothing to share. "New plan: make something up!"

I itched my nose with my middle finger, and they both burst into laughter. I joined them, grateful for their over-the-top banter. They knew exactly how to calm me down. "Thanks, both of you. I've got this." I did. From past experience, I knew all I had to do if things got weird was be my awkward self. That always sent the guys running.

But my sisters had never agreed, and they didn't now. "You *do* have this, Val. You absolutely do. You're gorgeous, ready, and safe. We'll do recon inside for you. There'll be at least one sweet, cute young guy here who'll thank his lucky stars for the chance to have a cheeseburger with you." Tori mimed eating a cheeseburger and thrusting at the same time.

She was always comparing sex with the men and women she dated to different foods. I'd asked her why, but she'd just told me I'd understand once I finally "tried a T-bone. Or a taco."

I wished I was attracted to tacos. Going home with a girl would feel a lot less intimidating.

Nessa groaned. "Tori, I'm telling you, if you think good sex is on par with eating a cheeseburger, you're not having it with the right people. Good sex is like chocolate fondue. *Great* sex is like the pastries at Chez Palette in Georgetown."

While they bickered, I breathed deeply, trying to get used to the smells that kept wafting past me. I didn't feel safe, but I knew I was. It was just really hard to remember, when the stench of what really could be alphas surrounded me. Alpha pheromones smelled every bit as awful as the combination of odors I was picking up now.

As an omega, I was more sensitive to scents, which was supposed to help me find a compatible mate. But I'd never felt safe around any alphas, except for a select few: my brothers and my bodyguards. And the guards weren't mate material. Like, they would lose their jobs and probably go to jail if they so much as kissed one of the "Paxson Princesses," as the press liked to call us.

Anyway, no alpha wanted an omega who was scared of her own shadow. Who couldn't even look him in the eye, much less hold a conversation. Which was one of the reasons I was doing this now. I had to stop being so afraid of everything.

I took a deep breath, held it, and let it out. I had this. I totally had this.

Then a burly alpha passed us by, smelling like moldy bread and lawn trimmings. He gave me and my sisters an assessing glance before he entered the club.

And suddenly, I was trembling again.

I had *nothing.*

I half-dragged my sisters a few feet away from the doors, closer to the curb. "I need to go back home. I'll t-try again next weekend." I'd be alone, but that was fine. I spent most of my time alone. I could bake. Maybe post the rhubarb fool recipe I'd been tinkering with. Finish the quilt I was making for my sister-in-law.

"No, no, *no*," Nessa wailed. "I'll be back at Denver U next weekend, and Tori will be at work." They'd taken time off to celebrate the New Year with our family, which had been more eventful than usual, with our eldest brother Nicky getting engaged. But the month was coming to an end, and my sisters both had lives to get back to.

Unlike me.

"And you'll be at home, Val." Tori's quiet words stopped Nessa's complaints. "You can go if you want. It's okay. But remember..."

I took another deep breath. I knew exactly why I had to stay. Just a few weeks before, my doctor had ordered me to stop taking the medicine I'd been on for my whole adult life. The heat suppressants, the oral-dose scent blockers, all of it.

After I'd revealed early as an omega, at sixteen, everything had gone wrong. I'd had twelve panic attacks the first year alone, and the doctors had decided it was safer for me to stay on suppressants year-round, and wait to have heats when I was older.

I'd known it couldn't go on forever. I'd been ducking my omega biology and hiding from the alphas of the world for almost five years now, even though my doctors had warned me the medication wasn't a permanent solution.

At the end of December, I'd started getting some of the side effects that were dangerous if they went on too long. Shortness of breath, rapid heart rate, vertigo... So my doctor had started tapering me off the mega-doses I'd been on for years. Now, I just took a pill once a day. It had been a slow process, since stopping all at once could throw me into a sudden heat.

Even thinking the word had my throat closing up. I would

lose my self-control, lose my ability to say no, and—if I didn't find a one-night stand beta *soon*—lose my virginity. Possibly to a hulking, barking alpha.

That idea terrified me so much, I started shaking. Of course, my sisters noticed. Nessa kissed the side of my hair, promising she'd stay by my side.

True to form, Tori stopped my panic attack with a lewd joke. "Come on, Val. This is my birthday present. You promised to give me your virginity."

I rolled my eyes. "I know. B-b-buy me a drink first, won't ya?"

A beta walking past right then stumbled and fell off the curb and lurched toward me, trying to grab onto something for balance as he slid in the ice-coated snow. I let out a small scream—not because I was scared, just startled, and I always reacted that way.

Like an idiot.

But before the beta could touch me, another man had inserted himself between us. The falling beta hit my protector and crumpled, as if he'd hit a mountain.

He might as well have. "You should be more careful, sir. You could have hurt the young lady."

The softly-spoken words sounded like a threat. No, like a *death* threat.

I shivered, but not from the cold. And not from fear.

The mountain stared down at the fallen man for a moment longer, assessing him, then sent a glance my way. "Did he touch you?"

I couldn't answer. I was busy memorizing the way the alpha's neck muscles flexed below his thick beard. I'd been doing that a lot, over the past few weeks. Trying to commit this particular body to memory. Trying to get a good whiff of him, even though all he smelled like was wet wool.

I cursed the inventors of chemical scent suppressors, and their diabolical brains. Of course, my brother was really to blame. Nicky insisted all our bodyguards wear scent blockers, especially the alphas, but only Donovan seemed to take the order seriously. I'd never once caught a hint of his true scent.

Damnit.

"He didn't lay one finger on her," Tori answered, "but if he did, would you tear off his arms and present them to Valentine as a birthday gift, Donovannnnn?" She sang out the name, while Nessa helped me over a patch of snow in my short, heeled boots.

Donovan didn't answer, but gestured for us to go past.

"Thank you, Donovan," Nessa said with a giggle. "We wouldn't want little Valentine here to miss the big night."

"Big night?" The words came out as if forced. Donovan had only spoken a dozen words in the past few weeks since he'd taken over as one of our bodyguards.

The man he'd replaced—a beta named Bobby, who'd been my guard since I was ten—had finally taken some of his stored-up vacation time, and was in Fiji with his boyfriend until the first of March. Bobby was friendly. Chatty. Of course, he'd helped raise me and my sisters, more or less. He'd been the one to refer Donovan, an old friend from his hometown of Aspen Springs.

I'd asked if we could just stick with one guard, Rufus, until the spring. I didn't like being around new alphas. But Nicky had insisted that the new hire was a perfect fit, though I didn't see why he thought that.

Donovan was... not friendly. He was stern. Severe. Huge, with a craggy face, a thick beard, and a nose that had been broken at least twice. His dark eyes were framed by thick lashes, but they were the only part of his face that could be called classically handsome.

But his body... I swallowed hard, just thinking about it. He was well over six and a half feet tall, and twice as wide as me. Larger than almost any man I'd seen, and all of it was muscle.

A small trickle of sweat rolled down my temple as I stared. His massive body had to have been transplanted from some Viking warship centuries before. For some reason, his size made me feel safe. And unsafe, too, but in a way I wanted to explore.

I'd glimpsed his abs once, when he reached to unload some skis off a roof rack. He was almost too well-defined, as if all he did in his spare time was lift heavier and heavier weights until his muscles popped out like rigid shelves.

Shelves I wanted to crawl up on and lick, just to see if he tasted as good as he looked.

My face grew too-warm in the cold air. Maybe I needed to take a second pill today.

"Big night?" he repeated, his voice slightly deeper, still not looking at me.

When it was obvious I wasn't going to answer, Tori took my arm and escorted me to the door of the club, unfastening my own puffy coat and revealing the borrowed cocktail dress I had on underneath. "It's our twenty-first birthday, and the night little Valentine's going to get her V card punched."

I glanced back at him, blushing. For a second, I thought Donovan was going to say something. Or maybe yell it. His whole face reminded me of a thunderstorm rolling in.

But all he did was clench his jaw, nod once, and tap his earpiece. "Is it a go?" He was talking to the other guard, who'd gone inside to make sure the club had our reserved table ready, and to check the exits. "Are you sure?" he said more softly, pretending he was talking in his earpiece, but now his eyes were locked on my face.

"Yes," I whispered. I was positive that I was ready to have sex.

It was just too bad that the only man I'd ever met who I wanted to do it with was eighteen years older than me, and my brother's employee. A man who had never touched me, hardly spoken to me, and probably thought I was a stupid kid.

"I'm ready." I dropped my eyes from his disapproving gaze and followed my sisters inside.

Chapter 2

Donovan

As an alpha, I lived my life constantly fighting for control.

No matter what it cost me, I knew I had to win that fight every day, and keep my alpha nature subdued. I was too strong, too powerful, to let the leash slip even the smallest bit. Especially around Valentine.

The idea that I could inadvertently hurt the young, fragile omega I was sworn to protect haunted me. If I was being honest, I'd admit that it filled me with fear.

I'd done it once before, after all—injured a woman. I would *never* let that happen again. But as I followed my young charge into the après-ski dance club, I was fully prepared to hurt any man who touched her.

And kill any man who thought he would take her home tonight and fuck her.

For the first time, I was grateful for my employer's restrictions on carrying a firearm around Valentine. Not because it triggered her panic attacks, but because even the thought of her with another man made me feel more than a little homicidal.

Within five minutes, I had a feeling the night would end in a bloodbath anyway, if I didn't get her out of here fast. The place was packed, mostly with hungry-looking men. Before I could get the girls' attention, a group of women, all wearing short dresses made out of sequins and sashes that made it clear they were there for a bachelorette party, engulfed the triplets, including them in their celebrations.

I shot a quick look at Rufus, the other guard on detail. He nodded, keeping watch on a group of too-drunk-for-comfort men at the bar, who were raking their filthy eyes over my girl... *our* girls.

Oh, who the fuck was I kidding? The sisters were Rufus's charges. Valentine was mine. She always had a dedicated guard, and I knew why.

She was the one the bastards of the world kept targeting. Her sweetness and innocence practically shone from her face, a lure the criminals of this world couldn't resist.

After I'd gotten the call from my boss at Storm Security, I'd read the file on Valentine Paxson that had been accumulating over the past decade and a half. The first abduction attempt had occurred when she was ten. The nanny had tried to take all three of the triplets, but only succeeded in snagging Valentine for seven long hours.

Supposedly, she'd come back unharmed. But Bobby Kenedy, the man who'd brought me in for the job, had given me the inside scoop. Something had happened that day to change a formerly funny, outgoing girl into a reclusive, frightened child.

And what had happened later had been every bit as bad. Other students at their private school had targeted her for the kind of bullying that was hard to prove, and harder to stop. It had begun with name calling, then a series of anonymous "pranks." It had ended in her quitting school entirely to be privately tutored along with her sisters until high school began.

But Bobby's quiet, verbal report of what had happened when Valentine—and only her, out of the triplets—revealed as an omega at the tender age of sixteen, was what made me want to burn down the world every time I thought of it.

It didn't matter if she was one of the richest girls in the world. Because she was an introverted omega, living in a world filled with grasping, cruel alphas, she had lost any hope of peace.

But I would do anything to make sure she never had to feel unsafe again.

"Donovannnn?" Planting herself in front of me, Tori called my name over the noise of the crowd, pulling me from my murderous thoughts. "Can you please get Valentine's purse from the car? She left it."

"No," I replied, my eyes tracking Valentine. She was seated at the bar, with a vacant stool on one side. Her sister sat beside her, but a group of weaselly beta males was already swarming, angling for the empty seat.

"She needs it," Tori insisted. "Please?"

"Why?"

Tori's response was almost too low to hear. "She may need her anxiety meds."

Anxiety meds? I had to force myself not to curse aloud. Why her sisters were encouraging her to do this, to rush into physical intimacy... No. If I allowed myself to think about what the purpose of this visit was, I'd lose my shit entirely.

If it were up to me, I'd haul Valentine's pretty, far-too-young ass out of this club, lock her in the kitchen where I'd noticed she was happiest, baking all that sweet shit she was obsessed with—or maybe in her room, where she spent most of her time, reading or sewing stuff—and tell her sisters to leave her the hell alone.

From the first moment I saw her, I'd understood why this

young woman would always be at risk, and it wasn't just her fortune. Anyone would want her. She was kind, quiet, gentle, and *good* in a way I'd never imagined a billionaire heiress would be. While the rest of her nine siblings were accomplished and admired, Valentine made it her goal not to be noticed, but to do small things that made everyone's lives easier.

I had listened as she quietly asked her siblings what cookies and cakes were their current favorites, then watched her sneak into the kitchen after everyone was fast asleep, and spend hours making them. She'd hand-woven scarves for the whole family for the holidays, making sure to use their favorite colors.

She was a listening ear to her sisters, laughing along with their stories about their exploits at work and school, not ever complaining that her own life was so small.

She asked about others' dreams, and hopes. I'd had the good fortune to watch over her during her twice-weekly volunteer "betasitter" visits to a low-income nursery near the triplets' shared apartment in Denver. The love she lavished on the babies there was only one of her gifts to them and their families, though as far as I could tell, none of them realized she actually provided all the funds for the center.

She was the reason twenty-two single parents were provided with free, top-notch childcare, so they could work full-time jobs. She was also the fill-in sitter who covered for the center's employees when they needed time off.

She was the one who made sure the city installed pedestrian crosswalks nearby, and routed a bus from there to the city center.

I had a suspicion she was also the reason a low-income apartment complex next to the center suddenly had a free, clean, fully furnished unit available whenever a new mother needed one.

Valentine Paxson was a saint, from what I'd seen, and she never asked for anything in return. But I could see what she wanted when she was holding the infants.

She wanted to be a mother.

I forced myself not to imagine her in my small kitchen, wearing nothing but an apron over her pregnant belly, a sprinkling of flour on her slender arms, leaning over to lick a droplet of batter off a spoo—*Fuck.*

Casually, I folded my hands over the damned erection that was tenting my pants.

"We'll stay right here," Tori promised, then wove her way through the crowd and plopped down on the empty stool, giving me a thumbs up.

I sighed, then spoke into my earpiece. "Rufus? I have to grab Valentine's purse. Do not let her go off with some asshole."

"You know she's twenty-one, Monk," he said, using the nickname the others had given me. They liked to joke that I'd taken a vow of celibacy. They weren't far off. But Rufus was the only one who openly mocked me about it. He was only a few years older than the girls, and in my opinion, more immature than any of them.

"Exactly. Too young for this place."

"Chill out, Father Donovan."

I stifled a growl. "Do you swear to keep eyes on them, on her, until I return?"

He let out an exaggerated sigh before he replied impatiently, "She's here to get laid, old man. She's going to go off with one of these guys."

"Not on my watch," I spat. Did this guy not *understand?* I turned on my heel and left the club before I helped him understand with a swift punch to the gut.

I should have been gone for less than five minutes, but some drunk idiot chose that moment to plow his Dodge truck into the back of our reinforced Hummer. I didn't give a shit about the minimal damage to the Hummer, but the guy was messed up. I took an extra ten minutes to make sure the head wound bleeding was superficial—it was—and to call the police and an ambulance.

I texted Rufus the news, and instructed him to escort the girls back in the hotel limo if they were ready to go before I got done. When he didn't reply immediately, I called.

He assured me they would be at the club for a while, since Valentine had gotten sick. "Puked all over some beta who bought her drinks. Classic Valentine," he joked, yelling over the thumping music in the background. "Don't worry. I'll take good care of the princesses."

"Fuck!" I kicked the Hummer's tire with my boot. I'd known she was nervous, but not puking nervous. I needed to get to her.

But first, I had to stop and wash the blood off me, since the paramedic had taken one look and assumed I needed a trip to the hospital as well. I had an extra shirt in the car, but not any of my other stuff—including the prescription-strength scent blockers I was required to wear at all times around Valentine.

When I'd first taken the job, I'd been given the option to take de-scenting pills, but the side effects were a bitch. So I used a ton of spray daily, reapplying anytime it started to wear off or washed off. It made me stink like wet wool.

The air around me now, though, was distinctly cedar and eucalyptus-scented.

Shit. I smelled like the alpha I was now, which was against my contract. More importantly, it might scare my charge. But I wasn't going back to Denver to get more.

The shitty, over-the-counter ones would have to do. I jogged to the 24-Hour Druggie, a combination marijuana dispensary and convenience store, and bought what I needed, then sprayed myself down. The whole time, my instincts were blaring an alarm.

But Rufus had promised to stay with her, with them. He had... *Wait.*

He hadn't promised that. He'd said he would take good care of them, like they were goldfish he'd won at a carnival.

Fuck.

By the time I ran back into the club with Valentine's purse in my hand, over forty-five minutes had elapsed.

And Rufus and the girls were gone.

Chapter 3

Valentine

"Valentine, are you done? Are you okay?" Tori was outside, blocking the ladies' room door, making sure no one came in.

The smell had gotten to me, just as I'd mustered the courage to talk to the cute beta guy who'd been hitting on me. We'd talked for a while, and he'd asked for my number, then hinted that he'd like to go home with me.

For once, a guy had looked right over Tori and Nessa, and wanted *me*. And what did I do? Threw up Midori all over his white Henley. He'd spilled his whole beer on me as he tried to avoid the spew.

"I want to go home," I mumbled to a waiting Nessa as I exited the restroom. I'd scrubbed the puke and liquor out of my hair in the sink, and off my arms and front. But my short dress was almost see-through now, and my nipples were doing their best to poke holes in the wet fabric. "I need my purse. I don't have my scent blockers."

"All you need are your phone and condoms. And Tori stuck half her supply in your coat pocket." Nessa pulled a lip gloss out of her tiny clutch and applied a dab to my dry mouth. "You know how we taught you that vomiting on a guy was a way to get rid of him? I never thought I'd say this, but somehow you made it sexy."

"Stop messing with me."

She grabbed my shoulders and gently spun me to see. "Look. Cutie McHotterson is still waiting for you. Only now he's waiting without a shirt. You have game I never knew existed, Valentine. You made *throwing up* irresistible."

I blinked, then blushed. The guy—whose name was Michael—really was there, standing by the bar with no shirt on, talking to Nessa. But as soon as I walked back to the bar, his eyes were on me, not her.

He grinned as I approached. "Hey, gorgeous. You're not sick?"

My face flamed, and I dropped my eyes. "No. Just humiliated."

He lifted my chin with two fingers. He really had nice eyes, green and crinkled at the corners, like he smiled a lot. "Hey, no need for that. Midori makes my stomach do the mambo, too. Want to dance?" The music was so loud, it was hard to hear him over the throbbing beat.

"I was thinking of going home," I admitted.

He winked and flexed his pecs at me. "Come on, birthday girl! The night's young. Maybe we could take the party somewhere a little quieter?"

"Um..." I checked my phone. Fully charged. I checked my courage.

Almost entirely empty.

He moved right in front of me, gently trailing a hand down my arm. I shivered, and tried to convince myself it was a good shiver. "Want to go back to the hotel with me?" Behind him, Tori was nodding her head and giving me two thumbs up.

"Don't worry, I gave your sisters my number. We're staying in the same hotel." He lifted an eyebrow. "Pretty sure one of them ran a criminal background check on me while you were cleaning up."

"You passed?"

"They said to tell you to be back in the room by midnight, and to have a cheeseburger or two. Are you hungry?"

I was panicky, and flattered, and weirdly disappointed. It was this easy to have sex? Like, you just walked into a club, had a drink, threw up on a guy, and boom! He was hooked?

My sisters were right. I'd built this up into a big thing, when it was more like going out for a cheeseburger. Casual. Not special, but not something to avoid.

"I should have had a cheeseburger years ago," I murmured, taking his arm.

"I'll get you one on the way home." Michael led me through the club, giving finger guns to some other guys in the corner. One of them made a check mark on an invisible board. I was about to pull away when he muttered, "Ignore those jerks. They're just jealous I've got the most beautiful woman in this place on my arm."

My phone pinged as I pulled on my coat, and I saw a string of texts—mostly eggplant emojis—from my sisters. Rufus was at the door, as usual, and he tilted his chin up at me. When he tapped his throat, I pulled my collar a little wider, showing the gold necklace with the tracker in it that I always wore. That earned me a wink. He crossed his arms over his chest and mouthed a word. *Condoms?*

I nodded, blushing harder. *In my coat,* I mouthed back. It was so awkward, with everyone knowing I was going to have sex.

Michael helped me into my coat, then pulled his over his

bare chest, flexing his pecs at me and winking again. "Like what you see, Vanessa?"

"I'm Valentine," I corrected.

Quickly apologizing for his mistake, he took my arm on the icy sidewalk. As we walked to his BMW, he talked non-stop about himself, not letting up even after we were on the road. I stared out the window as he drove, getting more and more nervous.

"So then the rowing team was one man short, and I was like, hey, I can fill the spot, I do CrossFit four times a—"

"Michael?" I interrupted. "I'm pretty sure the hotel was back there."

"Oh, I thought you wanted to eat?" he teased, but there was something off in his tone. "I know the best spot."

"Where?"

Before I finished the word, he'd pulled off the road and into a rest stop that was mounded with snow on both sides. I couldn't even see the main road from here, and when he switched the ignition off and pushed his seat back, I knew something was up.

His dick, apparently.

"Right here." He pointed at his crotch. "All a hungry girl like you needs to fill up."

"You've g-g-got to be k-kidding me." Damnit, my stutter was back. "T-t-take me back now, please."

"Come on, you know you want it," he said, unzipping his pants. "Suck me off now, and when we get to my place, I'll let you come."

I reached into my pocket for my phone, but it fell out of my shaking hand and clattered to the floor of the car, stuck between the seat and the gear shift. I half-leaned over to retrieve it, but that brought my head closer to his crotch, so I let it go.

"Come on, baby, don't tease." He paused, and made what he might have thought was a sexy face. It looked like he was constipated. "What is it? You need me to take charge? You like to be called a little slut? I bet you're kinky as fuck behind those sweet eyes."

"What?" I blinked as he whipped out his... Well, he didn't whip much out. It looked like a stumpy, pale mushroom. "W-why are you acting this way?"

"Jeez, drop the innocent act. You got me all worked up." He started jacking his cock, using two fingers.

I had the door open and was out of the car before he could finish the sentence, but not before he could come, judging by the noises he was making.

Leaving the club with him had been stupid. But getting out of the car, at least a mile out of the city, in the dark, in the snow, with no streetlights, and—after he revved the motor and sped off—no phone either? That redefined stupid.

But I knew what to do. I grabbed my necklace and pinched the heart-shaped pendant as hard as I could. All I had to do now was not stumble into a snowbank, or a half-frozen stream. Pretty much just not die, and I'd be fine.

Well, fine until my bodyguard caught up with me. I was going to be in so much trouble then.

Chapter 4

Donovan

Rufus answered his phone on the first ring. "Where is she?"

"Chill, Monk. She found a sweet, weak-ass little beta guy and is back at the hotel by now—"

"You're not with her? You didn't fucking *follow* her?"

"The girls got his information and ran it. He's a junior at Colorado State and has no priors."

As he spoke, I stormed back out of the club and headed for the Hummer. "Priors don't mean shit. There's a first time for everything." There was about to be a first time for me to kill a beta punk, if he touched her. "Those sisters of hers bullied her into this."

"Donovan, you're acting like a boyfriend, not a bodyguard. Do I need to talk to Mr. Halder about reassigning you?"

The little shit was acting like he'd had this job forever. He'd been hired three months before me, and I'd gotten the impression from a recent conversation with our boss, Storm Halder, that when Bobby returned from vacation, I would be offered

Rufus's spot. His lackadaisical attitude had been noted, even if he pretended he was a pro.

I forced myself to answer calmly. "I'm protecting her."

"She's allowed to have a life. She's allowed to have sex." I went silent, knowing what he said was true. But hating it. "Stop worrying, *Dad*. She promised to be back in the room by midnight. She's got her phone."

"Call me Dad again and I'll feed you your own teeth like popcorn, you little fuck."

I hung up as Rufus started swearing. Finally reaching the Hummer, I slid into the leather seat and started the engine. The girls all had tracker jewelry, but they'd talked their brother into making it only sound the alarms when either he or they activated them.

It was all I could do not to call Nicholas Paxson right then and tell him it was an emergency, but I knew I was overreacting.

She was fine. She was too young for me, but not too young for... for sex. Rufus had reminded me that I wasn't her boyfriend, or her dad. I had no right to tell her what she could or couldn't do.

But fuck, I wished I did.

I heard the steering wheel crackle under my grip, but then I heard something far more terrifying. My cell phone buzzed with a triple-tone alarm that could only come from one person.

My Valentine.

I had the app open and her position verified in seconds, and was on my way to the edge of town, making a mental list of who I was going to kill—the beta fuck and Rufus were at the top—as my focus narrowed on finding and protecting my omega.

If the GPS hadn't marked precisely where she was, I would have driven right past. She was huddled against a snowbank that indicated a deserted, dark rest stop. I hit the brakes and turned on the hazard lights, leaving the engine running as I raced to her side.

Snow was falling again, and I cursed when I got close enough to make out her pale face and reddened nose. She'd been crying. My throat was clogged with so many conflicting emotions, I wasn't sure what would come out if I spoke, so I didn't say a word. I just picked her up and carried her to the Hummer.

I'd never touched her before now, and our skin didn't come in contact, but the scent of her—vanilla and cinnamon, though it was sharp with notes of distress—traveled straight from my lungs to my heart, and wrapped around it.

She had never smelled like this before. I'd known she wore some sort of scent blocker, as most omegas did, but it was a crime to cover this. Her natural perfume was like breathing in one of the first mornings of the winter holidays, when the kitchen was rich with the scents of baking, and the house filled with laughter and joy, expectation and delight.

As I sat her on the back seat and pulled away, her ice-cold hand shot out and stopped me.

And the world stopped turning.

I gasped as a bolt of pure feeling—pure *bliss*—shot through me, and she echoed the sound. Her hazel-green eyes, red rimmed and tear filled, went wide, and her nostrils flared, trying to take in my scent. When she couldn't pick it up, her nose scrunched up, and her tiny, perfect face creased into a frown.

Thank god I'd picked up the scent blockers. If I hadn't, she would know what I did.

That she wasn't just my charge. She was my true mate. My omega.

My life.

And she'd been hurt. Maybe even... My alpha nature roared inside me, ready to find the one who had taken her and left her here in the snow, and tear out his heart for her. But her eyes were glassy and unfocused, as if she were going into shock.

Quickly, I shut the door behind me, closing us into the back seat together, then reached under the long bench for one of the blankets we kept there. Omegas were rare, but the Paxson family had more than their share, and when omegas had a bad day, they needed comfort. Which meant blankets, warmth, sweet foods and drinks, and safety. I'd added a few extra blankets to the stash, just in case.

My gut twisted as I wrapped one around her shoulders, covering her up almost entirely, then turned the heat to its highest setting.

"Th-thank you." Her whimpered words felt like a knife in my gut. She shouldn't thank me. I'd allowed her to be taken.

My voice trembling with rage and shame, I managed to ask, "Do you need a hospital? Valentine, sweetheart, are you hurt?" She shook her head slightly, after a slight pause. "Did he... Did he touch you? Did he—" *Fuck.* "We're going to the hospital." I tried to pull away, but her grip was surprisingly firm on my arm.

"No," she gasped, sucking in a quick breath. "He didn't even touch me. I'm just cold."

Shit. "You could have hypothermia."

Another head shake. "I was only out there for a few minutes. I don't want—I just need—"

I cupped her cold cheeks in my hands. "What do you need? Anything. I'll give it to you."

Her eyes met mine, and something sensual flared in her innocent gaze. "Take me home?"

I opened my mouth to answer. Did she mean the hotel? Her apartment in Denver?

My alpha nature had me growling at a third option. *Home to my cabin in Aspen Springs.* To my bed, for the rest of our lives.

But my phone rang. I knew the ring tone.

"Mr. Paxson, I have her. She's unhurt, but cold. She's asked to be taken home." I gave him a quick explanation of what had happened. Or at least, what I thought had happened.

He snarled. "I'll expect a full report in the morning, and your fucking resignation afterward. *How* could you let her be taken?"

I wasn't going to bother to explain myself. He was right. I had left my charge, and no matter what the circumstances had been, I deserved to be fired.

I sure as fuck didn't deserve her.

Suddenly the phone was snatched from my hand. And my world turned upside down again.

"Nicky, you will shut your... your *fucking* mouth right now and listen to me." I'd never heard little Valentine curse. I didn't like it.

But my cock did. Hearing that word fall from her lips was apparently all it took to have me rigid. I shifted, the position I was wedged into in the back seat becoming painful as my dick grew hard, and listened to Valentine quietly put her brother in his place.

"I went to a club with Nessa and Tori." She hesitated, and the dim interior lighting showed her face going a rosy pink. "I'm more or less off the suppressants. I needed a beta. Yes, needed. Dr. Grantham *prescribed* it." She closed her eyes, not looking at me. "Because I've never... had it." A longer pause. "Sex, you idiot. I've never had sex and I didn't want my first time to be in my heat. Or with an alpha."

His voice got quieter, his tone kinder, and I slowly exited the back seat, going back around to the front. My head buzzed with the knowledge that a doctor had prescribed... sex. What the hell kind of quack would do that?

Valentine gave her brother the explanation of all that had transpired since I left her to get her purse. Her reflection in the rearview mirror was defeated as she answered her brother's questions.

"No, don't tell the rest. Don't tell anyone. Not that anyone can c-call me," she muttered, then took a breath, calming herself. "That's why I had to use the necklace. My stupid phone fell between the seats of the jerkoff's Beemer... No, he didn't do any crime. I got out of his car while he had his hands full. Well, one hand, half-full." She cringed. "Yeah, sorry, TMI. I just want to go home now. Don't fire Donovan. I need him." She went quiet for a long moment. "I need him to take me home, okay? And..." Her eyes met mine in the rearview mirror. "I trust him, Nicky. I trust him with my life."

A long pause.

"No. He doesn't scare me. He would never hurt me."

My heart thumped.

She handed me the phone over the seat, and I spoke quietly into the receiver. "You heard that, Mr. Paxson? Someone needs to track her phone and send his details to the local police. He needs to be in jail *now*."

"Needs to be?" My boss's tone was lethal, his voice loud enough that every word he said could be heard clearly in the Hummer. "She said she wasn't hurt. Did he..."

"No, she's fine. She was cold, that's all. A little shaken."

"Then why does he need to be in jail?"

"Because he left her in the snow, on the side of the road. And it's the only place he'll be safe from me." The only thing that would keep me from murdering that fucking twit would be iron bars.

"Consider it done. Take her home, Donovan. Give her whatever she asks for, whatever she needs. She's fragile."

"I know."

"Don't forget it."

Chapter 5

Valentine

I'd never wanted a cheeseburger so badly in my life. My stomach was roaring to be filled. Or maybe it was a part of me a little lower needing the filling. Donovan's weirdly scent-free hotness was making me hungry. And thirsty.

That was an idea. I could order a bottle of water and spill it all over him. Discover if his scent matched his physique. Strong, robust, thick as his thighs... *Crap.* My panties were growing damp.

Who was I kidding? It didn't matter if he smelled like old tuna. I wanted to roll around in whatever smell he had until it coated me inside and out.

I didn't want a cheeseburger. I wanted *his* cheeseburger, all up in my bun.

I almost giggled, but my wild thoughts of washing Donovan down with water and my hands, to discover the natural scent he must have as an alpha, had me squirming in my seat. "What does a girl have to do to get a cheeseburger around here?" I mumbled aloud.

One thick eyebrow quirked up in the rearview mirror. "Are you buckled in?"

"I am now," I grumbled, knowing he wouldn't start driving until I'd done it. I'd already slipped my wet, uncomfortable boots off. But the seatbelt felt too tight as well, and I really didn't want to wear it. The part over my chest was smothering me. Maybe if I didn't unbuckle it, but just let the top part slide behind my back...

"Don't even think about it."

I froze. "Think about what?"

"About taking your seatbelt off. You're precious cargo."

"Cargo?" I sniffed. "Just what every girl wants to be called." The blanket he'd put around me was nice, but not enough. I pulled the seatbelt halfway over my head and moved around on the seat, reaching for the extra blanket that I knew was under the bench seat. I'd seen Donovan put a new one or two in the Hummer, and it had been all I could do not to take them out and build a mini-nest in the back seat. But my sisters would have teased me for eternity.

They had already been pointing out how Donovan stared at me, and took special care to open my doors first, and carry all my things. I'd reminded them it was his job.

But I'd wanted it to mean something. My inner omega had hoped for more. Suddenly, a wave of *need* washed over me.

More blankets would help. I slid farther out of the seatbelt, trying to get the third blanket that was just out of reach.

"Sweetheart, I'm warning you. If you don't sit that perfect little butt of yours down, there will be consequences."

"Consequences?" I blinked, trying to figure out what he meant.

But Donovan didn't reply. He just stared at the road ahead, his jaw clenching.

Had he meant he would spank me or something? And wait... he was calling me sweetheart now?

Something had changed. I thought back to the moment when I'd reached out and touched his hand. Our first touch. It had felt... significant. Like electricity.

My older sister Lindyann had met her true mate, and I'd read plenty of omega romances about finding "the one." They all said you'd know if you met your perfect match. But the scent was the only sure way to tell.

I couldn't be sure, without scenting him.

It was possible, though. What if this Viking, this enormous, terrifying-looking man was my true mate? The other half of my soul.

The thought made something inside me click, like a final puzzle piece being moved into place. I didn't have to wonder. Didn't have to smell him. He was mine. He had to be.

Wow. Somewhere, the universe was laughing, or drunk. There had never been a pairing as unlikely. I was scared of everything. And everyone with any sense was scared of him.

I threw the blanket off, feeling suddenly hot. But when the blanket hit the floor, something twisted inside. I struggled out of my coat and pulled the blanket back over me. "I need a damned cheeseburger." *And I probably need to take another suppressant,* I didn't say aloud.

"I'll get you anything you need," Donovan muttered, turning at the next intersection.

We rode in silence down the main drag. The clubs were still hopping, and I saw a car being towed away, the front of it crumpled.

"That's why I was late getting back to you. That drunk idiot plowed into the Hummer."

"Were you hurt?" I leaned forward, the seatbelt catching me. He growled, but I didn't lean back. "Oh my gosh, I smell blood! Are you injured?" In a flash, I'd unbuckled my seatbelt and was climbing over the back of his seat to check on him.

"Damnit, Valentine!" He had the Hummer pulled over to the curb before I could find where he was cut. "I told you to *stay buckled.* Get back in your seat!" he half-barked at me.

It wasn't a command, not one I would have to obey. But it had sounded so angry, had reminded me of... I froze, my heart racing so fast, I thought I might pass out.

"D-d-don't–do not d-do..." I was hyperventilating, but I could tell from Donovan's soft cursing that he regretted using that hint of his alpha bark. "You–you're n-n-not allowed," I stammered. I knew Nicky had written that into the contract of every alpha who worked for our family and might come into contact with me. None of them could use their alpha bark in my presence, and if they did, it would be seen as an attack.

"Ah, sweet girl. I'm so sorry; I didn't mean it. I shouldn't have done that. I won't ever do it again; never again, I promise," he soothed, pulling me carefully over the seat and cradling me, half on his lap, his hands on my flushed cheeks. "I promise," he repeated, his face only inches above mine. "In and out, sweet-heart. Breathe with me."

I kept trying to find the words to explain why I'd freaked out. "B-b-blood—"

"It's not my blood, sweetheart," he explained once I'd managed to get my breathing under control. Well, if under control meant sort of quietly freaking out. "It was the guy who hit the car; he cut his head. He's fine, though they sent him to the hospital. It got on me, and I had to wash off and change my clothes." I breathed for another long minute, until he asked, "Better?"

"Much," I said, truthfully. I buried my face in his shirt, trying to scent him, but only picking up a slight trace of cedar underneath the laundry detergent and the scent-blocking spray.

I felt his breath in my hair, then a feather-light pressure as he rested his face on my head. One of his hands started smoothing my hair behind my ear, and goosebumps rose up on my arms. "I wish I c-could smell you."

"You know I signed a contract. I'm not allowed near you without blockers."

"But what if," I whispered, hoping my courage didn't fail me. "What if I liked your scent..." I wanted to tell him what I suspected. But my own scent was filling the vehicle. If we were true mates, wouldn't he have said something?

Wouldn't it be impossible for him not to touch me, kiss me, make me his?

"Shush, sweetheart." He lifted me up like I weighed nothing, settling me into the passenger seat—which suddenly seemed ridiculously far away—then buckled me in and put the car into gear.

"Where are we going?"

"To get a cheeseburger, and then to take you home."

"Not hungry?" Donovan asked a half hour later. We'd found an open fast-food restaurant, and he'd bought me the food I'd requested, not even allowing me to pay for it, even though I had my purse now. I'd felt flushed, so I'd taken half of another suppressant. I figured it was fine since I'd thrown up earlier, and I was supposed to take it with food, but the smell of the burger was turning my stomach.

Or that could have been the silence in the Hummer. It was just him, and me, and the fact that he wouldn't talk to me. As if he hadn't felt what I had.

What if he hadn't?

I hadn't had the guts to spill my soda down the back of his

neck, or do something equally extreme to get his attention, though I'd considered it. And I wasn't hungry anymore. The cheeseburger was half-unwrapped, growing cold and stale on my lap.

"This is the worst cheeseburger in the world," I muttered. "Kinda tempted to roll down my window so I can throw it out."

"Not a good idea," he replied gently. "If you throw food near the highway, a scavenger might get hit trying to carry it off the road."

I had a sudden vision of a raccoon dying because of me. Maybe a whole family of them. "Oh. That's... thoughtful. But I can't stand the smell. You want it?" I offered it to him. The corner of his lip twitched, and he shook his head once.

"I'm a vegetarian."

"You are *not*," I said, shocked. "You can't be."

"Why not?" The lip twitched again.

"Because you're—well, look at you!" I gestured to his massive torso. The Hummer had a larger than usual steering wheel, but it almost looked like a toy car under his hands. "Those thighs weren't built from celery sticks. All that meat had to come from somewhere!" I gulped. "Not that I've been looking at your meat. At least, not in the way my sisters use the term. I meant the meat on your bones. All of them. They have meat on them. So much meat." My voice trailed off, ending in a hoarse, humiliated whisper.

"What did you say?"

I slapped a hand over my mouth, not trusting what might come out. Who had I become? Was I channeling my sisters?

I was almost certain I had as many dirty thoughts as they did, but I never, ever said them out loud. Maybe my soda had been drugged. I tried to read the label. "No sodium pentothal," I muttered. "Does that say THC-infused? Ugh, Colorado puts pot in everything now. I think I'm high."

For a moment, the space between us was quiet. And then I heard a sound I had never thought I'd hear.

Laughter. Donovan threw his head back and... guffawed, that was the word. From the shock and surprise in his eyes as he made the sound, he didn't laugh often.

"You sound high, sweet girl," he said at last, then cracked the window a little bit. "Better eat some of that meat." I would have sworn he wiggled an eyebrow, but it was so fast, I couldn't be sure.

I turned my burning face to the window, letting the cold air rush over me. It felt so good on my heated skin, but soon, I was shivering again, and he rolled it back up.

Another half hour passed in silence. Well, I was contemplating the practicality of locking myself in a room for the rest of my life, where I would never have to face this man, or any man, or remember this moment.

It was the low point of my life. Well, so far.

In the next hour, that low point dropped... along with the remainder of my inhibitions.

Chapter 6

Valentine

I was drowsing in the car, dreaming of going down a slip-and-slide in the backyard of my house, with Donovan holding onto me the whole way, both of us naked and his knot pressing deep inside me, when a groan woke me up.

"Sweetheart? Whatever you're dreaming about, you need to stop."

"What—" My eyes snapped open as I realized what had felt like a waterslide in my dream was the front seat of the Hummer. "Did I spill my soda?" I mumbled, before I took a breath and realized the liquid that was all over the bottom of my thighs wasn't soda.

It was slick. My own juices, spilling out of my panties.

"Oh my god, I'm so sorry. This is so humiliating," I began, grabbing for the stack of napkins on the center console. But before I could use them, another gush of warmth flooded out of me, accompanied by a searing pain in my abdomen.

Why wasn't the pill working? I peeked at the clock on the console. It had been over an hour. It should have taken effect.

"I'm... I'm dying. Donovan, hospital," I croaked. "My stomach..."

"What's wrong?" he demanded, his voice hoarse. "Food poisoning?"

I stifled a groan, then tried to speak through the pain. "No. It's my heat. I'm having a heat."

My doctor had told me I should have at least three months before the first one hit. I had time to taper off the suppressants. Time to lose my virginity with a beta. I didn't want my vaj to be torn apart with some monster knot.

Searing pain zipped up my spine, of all places. Why hadn't anyone warned me that heat cramps felt like being stabbed with knives all over? I whimpered through the next sharp wave, the sound of Donovan's cursing distracting me a bit.

"What do you need, Valentine? What do you usually do for your heats?"

"I've never had one," I gritted out. "This will be my first."

The car's engine was the only sound, as Donovan held his breath. Then he muttered, "Of fucking course." The air inside the Hummer filled with an odd scent, like burning cedar.

I breathed it in, oddly comforted. "I've been on suppressants since... since I was sixteen. But the doctors said it's dangerous. They were worried about my heart, my valves getting weak. So I had to stop."

"That's why you went to that club, isn't it?"

"Yes. I didn't want to, but I don't have a choice. If I d-don't get my body back on track—" I groaned as another sharp cramp doubled me over.

"So no doctors?"

"They'd just send a heat-trained orderly in to fuck me, I'm pretty sure," I half-joked, half-sobbed. Once this wave of pain passed, I'd take another one of the mild suppressants in my purse. A whole pill this time.

But I had a feeling it wouldn't be enough.

"No hospitals, okay? N-n-no... strangers."

The burned cedar scent grew stronger. "Okay, baby. It should only be another two and a half hours to your apartment, but the roads are icy, so I have to go slow. It could take four, or even five. I'm going to pull off and get some things for you. You can use them in the car on the way."

I wanted to crawl under the seat and hide. I knew what he meant. Sex toys. Sure enough, when he pulled off the highway and into a parking lot in front of a neon-covered store that said *24-Hour Adults Only Toys and Dispensary* on the sign, I started crying.

"Hey, baby, stop now." A finger wiped away my tears. Out of nowhere, all the blankets from under the back seat were on my lap, and strong hands were wrapping me up in them. "You stay here, and I'll go get some things that will help."

"Don't leave me," I gasped. But he put his hands on both sides of my face and angled it up to his.

"I'm locking you in, and I'll be back in less than five minutes. I want you to hold my phone up to your ear. If you need me, just tap the screen here. This is the app to speak directly into my earpiece. I can drop everything and run back."

I held his phone up to the side of my face, wondering why it smelled ever so slightly like my favorite spa. Eucalyptus and cedar. It felt safe and relaxing, even after he'd disappeared into the store.

I pressed the phone to my cheek, then darted my tongue out to lick the side of it, where the scent was strongest. I licked a little harder, tasting it, knowing I was being weird. I didn't care; no one could see in the tinted windows.

Time seemed to stretch as the cramps came faster and faster, and I babbled my thoughts out loud, the sound of my own voice keeping my mind off the pain. "I'm so scared—no,

I'm terrified of this stupid heat. I don't have any idea what to expect... *Ah!*" I panted through the pain, then kept on babbling aloud, the noise in the Hummer's interior distracting me from the waves of agony. "None of the Omega League videos I watched at home covered cramps that feel like being sliced open with swords from the inside."

Of course, none of them would've imagined an omega would need to tackle a five-year-overdue heat. They for sure hadn't had a pamphlet on what sex in a delayed heat would be like, especially for a virgin.

And I was one hundred percent a virgin. Nothing besides my own fingers had ever been inside me, except a few slender tampons I'd used for the few periods I'd had before my sixteenth birthday had ushered in my new biology.

My sisters had tried to get me to play with toys for years, warning me that I needed to know what to do when the time came. What I liked. But I'd been stubborn, and scared.

Anyway, the suppressants I'd been on had killed any sex drive I might've had. Every time I'd thought about using the dick-shaped devices on myself, I'd felt slightly ill.

Sure, I'd used my hands. I'd had orgasms, or at least I thought so. They never felt like what the romance novels said, though. They took a long time to happen and reminded me of a soda pop with not enough fizz.

"Until Donovan. He's got all the fizz I could ever want. I'd drink him down like a cream soda... No, stop thinking about him like that, Valentine. He doesn't want you. Nobody wants the stupid, awkward, painfully shy omega who can't even orgasm right."

My heart ached as I pressed my lips together, letting the Hummer fill with silence at last, though my thoughts were every bit as noisy in my head.

What was I going to do? I'd never had a heat, not since the

first one... I refused to think about that nightmare. The alphas who'd scented me at my high school, who'd shoved me into the boy's bathroom, barked and barked to keep me quiet, and torn my panties off. If it hadn't been for my necklace back then, I would have been...

Panic began to overwhelm me. I couldn't do this. Not alone. I fumbled for my necklace, almost pressing the heart, then remembered.

I had Donovan's phone. I looked for the button he'd shown me, then blinked. It was already connected, a wet patch of saliva on the spot he'd shown me.

I'd... licked the app open?

"Did you hear any of that?" I whispered.

There was no answer. Maybe he hadn't. I set the phone down a moment before a soft knock on the door alerted me to his return.

"What did you *buy*?" I breathed as Donovan put an enormous plastic bag filled with what had to be half the store inside. "Or what did you not buy?"

"Don't you worry about that," he grumbled, handing a sleek box to me. "I washed that one in their bathroom and used the sterilizing spray. The clerk said it should give you some relief until you can... Anyway, it's guaranteed to work." His cheeks flushed dark over his beard.

Horrified and intrigued, I opened the box and saw what he'd given me. "The Pussy Pounder 4.0?" I read aloud. "Guaranteed to d-deliver the best 'orgams' ever." I almost smiled. "Pretty solid guarantee. I've never had an 'orgam.'"

He made an annoyed sound. Annoyed at the typo, or at me? Probably me. Irritated that he had to do this kind of errand.

I focused on getting the toy out of its box. It was what my sisters called a starter vibe, a long purple wand with a tiny pair of rabbit ears on one end that were supposed to go on either side of the clit.

"I... I can't—" My next words were strangled, but Donovan cut a sharp glance my way.

"My job is to keep you safe, Omega. To guard you from anything that could hurt you, even your own biology. This isn't about sex. It's about your health. Put that under the blanket. It's got batteries."

"It's got a remote control." I pulled the matching purple control out. When he lifted an eyebrow, I held it out to him.

He swallowed. "Princess? What are you doing?"

I had no idea. "I don't want to lose it," I murmured, then ducked my head under the blanket when he took it.

"Four more hours of hell," I thought I heard him say, but then he repeated himself, louder, "Four more hours to go."

Chapter 7

Donovan

I was in hell, and not only because my true mate was trying to oh-so-quietly work a narrow dildo into her pussy on the seat next to me.

Or at least, that's what I assumed she was doing from the sounds. I couldn't be sure what was going on, not without ripping the blanket away from her and seeing her, touching her, helping her... *No.* I wouldn't help her plunge a plastic cock inside her.

That was my fucking job.

Except it wasn't. My literal job was to keep her safe, not to touch her intimately. But to do that, I had to ignore the roaring in my mind, the aroma of her arousal in my nostrils, and the steel length of pipe in my damned pants.

My eyes flitted to the remote control she'd handed me. If I used that, I wouldn't be touching her. I'd be controlling her pleasure, but not technically touching her. My fingers twitched on the wheel.

Kill that thought, Donovan Heart. Kill it, bury it, and cover the hole with cement. I'd warred with my own impulses for so long, I knew better than to give in, even a little.

My cock was harder than it had ever been in my thirty-nine years, and my balls ached like they'd been kicked by a horse. I didn't even want to think about my knot. Mine was a grower, not a shower—it was usually a slight swelling at the base of my too-thick cock, and only inflated to its full, super fucking problematic size when I was knotted inside a woman.

Not that I'd tried that since my first failed experience with knotting twenty years before. I forced myself to remember that day, the sound of the woman crying. The feeling of my own helplessness.

Ah, there was nothing like a little PTSD to kill an erection. My cock half-deflated almost instantly, and when I heard a tiny sob emerge from the blankets next to me, I went completely soft. "Sweetheart? What's happening?"

Her reply was muffled. "It's what's *not* happening. I can't do it."

"You can't..." I stopped my words so fast, I almost bit my tongue. "Why not?"

Not that I needed to ask. When I'd heard her mumbled monologue in my ear while I shopped for her, I'd almost passed out. Knowing that she'd never been touched, had never even desired anyone until me, had me planning all the ways I wanted to show her how her body worked. How we would work together, to make her feel better. Touch each other.

Not that I was an expert either, but I knew enough.

"I'm not g-g-good at it." Her weeping got louder. My inner alpha was growling at me to pull over and take over for her. Not with the remote control, or the vibrator, but my tongue and hands and teeth. Show her just how perfect she was, and how hard she could come, how many times.

I took a deep breath through my mouth, tasting her now-slightly-burnt cinnamon scent. "When we reach your apartment, you'll have all the time in the world to figure it out. You'll get good."

"Alone?" Another sob that felt like a rip in my heart.

"I'll stay on guard outside. I won't leave you unprotected."

"But I'll be by myself. That's all I'll ever have, isn't it? Lonely heats with plastic dicks and pretend knots."

"You can find someone—"

She made a frustrated sound. It was fucking cute. "I've *tried*. I'm practically a hermit. I tried with guys when I was homeschooled, friends of my sisters. They said I was defective. Frigid."

"You are not defective," I spat. "And only shitty lovers ever speak the F word."

There was a long pause. "Are you a shitty lover?"

I mock-growled. "You really are being a brat, aren't you? And here I always thought you were such a good girl."

She sucked in a breath, and the vehicle filled with a burst of bright, warm cinnamon scent. Of course she had a praise kink. She'd never had anyone tell her how perfect she was.

The dirtiest part of me, deep inside, whispered, *She never had a Daddy either. Maybe we can fix that.*

Damnit. Now my dick was harder than ever.

I started thinking about doing my taxes, unclogging toilets, roadkill, anything just to keep from coming at the thought.

She grumbled, moving the blanket around—probably soaking up her slick—before she poked her head out. Her hair was tousled, her eyes slightly swollen from crying. "Maybe I'm not a good girl. Maybe I have hidden depths."

"I'm sure you do." I forced what I hoped was a friendly smile. "You're so young, Valentine. You have years to explore your hidden depths. To find the right someone to invite into your bed, your nest, your heart."

"But I don't *have* time," she panted, her cramps obviously tearing through her again. "Donovan, even if I go to the hospital and use one of the heat orderlies, I can't do this with a stranger. I can't." Her eyes burned a hole in my cheek. "Donovan, would you... *Please*, would you help me?"

My mouth went dry. "I can't. I signed a contract. I gave your brother my word. He's my employer, sweetheart, and you're my responsibility. I may not be a good man, but I try to have integrity. I keep my word. Please don't push."

Her breath came out shaky, but she said, "I won't. But I want you to know... I think you're a good man. And I want you."

I want you. Those three words melted into me, soaking like water into my dried-up heart.

I'd heard them a thousand times over the years, from women who wanted to fuck me. They'd always come from women who'd seen me as a notch on a bedpost. They wanted me like they wanted a possession, or a toy, or a story to tell their friends about the huge, ugly alpha they'd spent the night with. Some of them wanted the challenge of being the one to tempt the "monk" into bed.

But that wasn't how Valentine said them. The way she said them made them sound like three other words. Words I knew I'd never hear from her lips.

"Please," she whimpered, then cried out again.

The road sign ahead was hard to make out in the increasingly heavy snowfall, but I knew this exit like the back of my hand. I'd taken it well over a thousand times.

I turned on my indicator, then took the off-ramp, following muscle memory as I drove into Aspen Springs. In ten minutes, we were at my cabin. I slung the bag of recent purchases on one arm, then got out and opened the door on Valentine's side. "Come on, sweetheart. Let's go inside and get you cleaned up." I lifted her, feeling the damp spot on the bottom of the blanket.

"I'm so embarrassed."

"You can't be. Burritos don't get embarrassed."

"B-burritos?"

I carried her to the front door, pressing my thumb against the lock pad there. One of the perks of working for Storm Security was a massive discount on all their latest tech, and I'd taken full advantage of it. "Yes, little burrito. Didn't you notice the blanket you're in?" I flicked on the light and carried her inside, using one foot to shut the door behind us. It automatically locked.

The room smelled a little like coffee, and I wondered if I'd forgotten to empty the machine the last time I was here. Which was... four weeks ago, now. I hadn't taken a day to come home since I got the call to fill in for Bobby.

I wouldn't lie to myself about why that was. I hadn't been able to leave her side since I met her. Long before I knew she was my true mate.

"What is this?" Valentine's hands moved over the blanket, noting the variations in color. "Is this..." She giggled. "Is this blanket actually a tortilla?"

"Good eye," I said. "It was a birthday gift from my sister last month."

"You have a sister?"

"I do. Rita Heart-Williamson. She's three years older than me." I stared down at her face. She had never looked so young, blinking up at me like a kitten. The green flecks in her hazel eyes shone like emeralds in the light, and her skin practically glowed.

"Her last name... Your last name is Heart? How did I not know that?" I shrugged, then felt my knees go weak as she said, "If we were mates, my name would be Valentine

Heart." She blushed so pink, it reminded me of cotton candy.

"Valentine," I said, my tone chastising, though my mind was playing those four words on repeat: *if we were mates.*

She changed the subject. "So she's forty?"

"Forty-two, princess. I'm thirty-nine. Old enough to be your father."

"Whatever. Old enough to be my..." She chewed at her bottom lip and turned away, her face reflected in the window. I watched her lips move, though she didn't speak aloud, and could have sworn she said, *Daddy.*

I'd never felt like such a lecherous alpha in my life. "Your heat has cooked your brain, sweetheart. I'm too old to be flirting with."

"You're pretty much the same age as my big brother, and his new mate is only a few years older than me." She sniffed, craning her head to look around. "Is this your house? It smells amazing!"

"Like old coffee?"

"No, more like a spa." She wriggled to get down, and the blanket fell to the ground when I let her go, making a slapping sound when the wet part hit the hardwood floor. "Oh, god, that's horrifying. Could you get me a mop?"

"Why don't I get you a change of clothes? It looks like your heat may be abating." I hoped so. I needed to get her home safe, sound, and still a damned virgin. And it was getting harder with every breath I took, every small, innocent touch. Every blush.

She covered her pink cheeks with her hands. "I hope so. Where's the guest bathroom?"

I pointed down the hallway. "There's only one, but it's yours. Take a shower and wrap up in a robe—I'm pretty sure there's a smaller one that my sister wears on her visits. I'll make something for us to eat." I checked the time. "It's almost three in the morning, but you didn't eat your burger. You need something in your stomach before you go to sleep."

"Something vegetarian?"

"I don't have any meat here." I laughed as her gaze dropped to the half-hard bulge in the front of my trousers. "Stop staring, sweetheart, or you'll make it worse."

She made a small squeaking noise, then scooted to the bathroom. I took the moment to adjust myself, and adjust the thermostat. Then I carried the bag of toys to the bedroom.

There were two bedrooms, but the guest room was small and utilitarian. No windows, and only a small table, a chest with my extra blankets, and a queen mattress on the floor. She'd hate that. I didn't have any omegas in my family, and I'd hardly even spoken to one until I'd been hired by Nicholas Paxson. But I'd taken the required classes back in high school, and I'd been reading every scrap of information I could on them since I met her.

Valentine would want a soft bed. Luxurious things. Omegas loved soft fabrics and fancy shit. I racked my brain to think of what else. Hot cocoa and chocolates...

I cursed at how little fresh food was in the house, while I rummaged through the kitchen, trying to think what I could cook for her that would be light enough for this late at night, and good enough for my omega.

Worthy enough for my little forbidden mate.

I stood in front of the open pantry door, my focus on her, as always. Listening to the water run, fighting not to imagine what she looked like in my shower, naked.

My scent was beginning to seep out of my pores as her shower went on, so I stepped into the mud room and sprayed myself down with the de-scenter, before making sure the cabin was locked up.

It wasn't anything like the places Valentine had lived. It was small and functional, remodeled to suit a bachelor who spent most of his time working jobs all over the world. It was only last year that I'd decided I had enough money saved to retire from the dangerous work, and spend the rest of my life in Aspen Springs. I would read, volunteer at the local fire department, maybe. Finally finish writing the novel I'd been dreaming up for a decade.

Until the call from Bobby came in, asking me to do one more short-term, local assignment. When I met the one I was hired to guard? All my plans crumbled.

When the water stopped, she called out, "Donovan? Is it okay if I lie down? My stomach still hurts."

She had no idea. She could ask me for anything in the world, and my answer would be yes. Anything except to hurt her.

"Of course. Use the big bedroom on the left when you come out," I called back. It wasn't until I heard the door to my bedroom close behind her that I realized my mistake.

My soft bed, with all the pillows and blankets? Even after four weeks away, it would still smell like me.

I was so fucked.

Chapter 8

Valentine

The shower had been a good idea. I'd washed all the embarrassing slick away, then bundled the wrecked blanket into the dirty laundry, even though a part of me had wanted to carry it around, since it had a hint of that lovely spa scent on it. Though the whole house had it, too. I'd need to ask Donovan what air freshener he used.

Now I was clean, and only a bit tired. I'd also taken another pill, though I knew that wasn't safe. Still, it was an emergency. I'd have to tell my doctor later.

The cramps had eased somewhat, even if I hadn't been able to have an orgasm in the car, or in the shower, even using the fancy detachable shower head. I was almost glad.

Sure, Donovan had been helpful and kind. But he'd made it clear I was a client. Not old enough. And even if I had a suspicion we could be true mates, he had smelled me in the Hummer and hadn't reacted any more than any alpha might. He hadn't said anything about my scent, or even tried to touch me more than he had to.

He hadn't tried again since carrying me inside, even though

my fingers had been itching to caress the harsh lines of his face, his body, ever since. I needed to drill it into my own head that even if he did make me feel safe, I wasn't anything more than a job to him.

I'd almost convinced myself that I'd imagined the touch that had sparked in my imagination, until I walked into his room and sat on the bed.

I had on a silky robe that I'd found in the towel cupboard and nothing else, since my underwear hadn't been salvageable. But the mild aromas of the shampoo, and the laundry detergent on the robe, were overwhelmed by a new scent as soon as I sat on the bed. Cedar and eucalyptus, a little stale, but still potent, rose in a haze of masculine scent from the bedding.

The smell I loved more than anything else in the world pulled me into the downy comforter, and I buried my face in it, sucking up great lungfuls of it, delirious with a rush of lust.

And then pain.

My slick was already flowing again, dampening my thighs, but the cramps were less painful than my heart when I realized what this meant.

"Valentine?" I lifted my eyes to the open doorway. He stood there, a remorseful expression on his face, his hands in fists at his sides. "I'm sorry. I should have changed the sheets. Sprayed them down."

He may as well have torn my heart out. He was sorry... about the sheets, or that he was my mate? Or both?

All my thoughts tumbled together. "You had scent-blocking spray on. But... but I didn't. You knew. You *knew* we were true mates, and... *Oh.*" I curled my nails into my palms, wishing there was any pain in the world that could distract me from the tearing feeling in my heart.

"I didn't know until tonight. Your perfume... I suspected. But I didn't know until—"

"Until I was off the suppressants, and you touched me," I finished for him. "And then you tried to hide it. You were so careful. You don't want me, do you?" He flinched. "Of course you don't. Why would you?" He took a step toward me, opening his mouth to speak, but I held up a hand. "Please leave. I have the toys, thanks to you. I'll handle my heat alone."

I slid off the bed, my back to the door, moving toward the bag. I didn't have any intention of using them—there was no way I could reach some mythical climax when my heart was bleeding out inside me—but I hoped it would spur him to get out and shut the door, so I could cry alone.

I'd cried alone so many times that I'd gotten good at being quiet. I was pretty sure my sisters knew how often I broke down, but... *Shit*. I needed to call them. They'd be worried about me.

I heard the door close and almost cursed aloud. Now I would have to go out there and face Donovan again. I had no choice.

I wasn't in the habit of swearing, but Nessa and Tori called them power words, and had informed me that sometimes, only a power word would do. This was surely one of those times. "Fuck," I muttered.

"Sweetheart, you shouldn't use that kind of language," a gravelly voice said, right behind me. Inside the room.

I squeaked and jumped up, feeling hands on my arms. Huge hands, moving from my wrists until they wrapped entirely around my biceps, pushing the robe up slightly as he trailed his fingers up my arms. The lightning feeling shot through me again, but muted now. "I asked you t-to leave," I said, proud that I was holding my ground.

"I'm not going anywhere, baby girl," was all he said.

"I need your phone." I cleared my throat, trying to dislodge the sex kitten that had gotten stuck in there. Honestly, I never sounded throaty and needy. "I have to call my sisters."

"That's a good idea," he agreed. "And I need to take a shower. Then we'll talk." When he let go of me, I slumped to the bed, fighting to ignore the new cramps that had started up like a series of pain-quakes in my uterus. Silently, he handed me his phone, unlocked it, and left the room.

My sisters' numbers were programmed in, and I chewed at my lip, unsure which one to call. I couldn't text; they knew I did that when I was trying to hide things from them. The amount of stammering I did was their clue to how I really was, so they always insisted on calling when the conversation was going to be intense.

Tori was more likely to come barreling down the road with a dozen Marines she'd convinced to murder Donovan. Nessa was slightly saner when it involved people hurting me, or even my feelings. But only slightly.

Nessa, then. I held the phone up, listening to it ring. She picked up instantly.

"Donovan, where *are* you? We were freaking because Val wasn't answering her phone, and then Nicky called and said that little shit-turd Michael was in jail, and she was—"

"It's me, Nessa," I interrupted. "I'm with Donovan."

"Oh, thank god! Where are you? Are you safe? Are you hurt? Nicky said you weren't well—"

"I'm fine. Mostly."

"Hang on," Nessa half-shouted. I heard a click as she turned her phone's speaker on, and suddenly Tori was blaring in my ear.

"We will never forgive ourselves, Val. *Never.*"

"Stop." I sighed as they didn't, just filled the line with a chorus of apologies, until I lost it. "Stop!" I yelled. "I need help."

"Anything."

I took a few calming breaths, then let it all spill out. "Donovan is my true mate."

They both gasped, and I told them about the touch, and the trip here, and how I'd realized the truth of who he was to me, from the bedding. "I was going into heat, and he still wouldn't touch me. He bought me a giant bag of sex toys, b-because he d-doesn't... d-d-d-doesn't want m-me." I didn't love how much I'd stuttered, but I was proud I hadn't fallen apart, getting it out.

"Donovan?" Tori breathed. "Incredible Hulk-caveman-bodyguard Donovan, who stares at you so much while you sleep that our other brothers told Nicky about it and said he should be fired, and a restraining order filed? The bachelor alpha who has the world's biggest crush on you, but won't act on it because he's an employee—*that* Donovan?"

"They reported him to Nicky?" I squeaked, shocked I hadn't heard of any of this.

"Yeah, supposedly Nicky told them Donovan was practically a monk. Not one relationship in decades. Not even a single lover over the past ten years, nothing that he could find. Nicky thought he was asexual; that's why he hired him."

"You asked about him?"

"Well, yeah. Once we noticed how he stared at you, and how you were always trying to get a whiff of him..."

Nessa broke in. "Do you remember the rock you tripped over on the walk outside the Lodge at New Year? When you fell and cut your palms? Donovan hired a crew and spent an entire night replacing the sharp rocks with little, soft pea gravel. The man is *obsessed* with you, Valentine. He's exactly what you need."

Tori hmphed. "If you like that silver fox, Viking, stern Daddy vibe."

The line went silent, and then to my shock, we all burst

into laughter. We had amassed a collection of every single type of age-gap romance—from sweet to more-than-slightly depraved—and they knew it was my favorite trope. Both my sisters had teased me about wanting to call a man Daddy. They hadn't known how right they were.

"Of course I like it." I sighed once they'd mostly stopped giggling. "But I'm not the problem."

"Then what is?"

"He doesn't want me. I'm too young, and he signed Nicky's contract."

"Oh, we can fix that. We'll tell Nicky what's going on—"

"No!"

Nessa argued with me for a moment, then asked about the bag of sex toys, which she dubbed the best birthday present ever, and chattered in a way that was beginning to seem suspiciously like she was filling time... until Tori cleared her throat.

"Ah, Val? Nicky says he would like Donovan to call him. Now."

"You *didn't*."

Of course she had. And she didn't apologize, just went on about true mates, and Nicky being understanding since he'd found his.

"I will never forgive you," I whispered.

She blew a raspberry into the phone. "You will. Anyway, I didn't call Nicky. I called Candy, and she took care of it."

I buried my face in my hands. "Does everyone know?" The line went silent. "Okay, I'll tell him to call." Hanging up the phone, I carried it out of the bedroom. The shower wasn't running, and I took a moment to look around.

I could see the kitchen through an open doorway, and the shine of white quartz countertops and a bright yellow stove made my feet itch to explore it. But I resisted, walking around the main living room first. The furniture was minimal: a

58

comfortable-looking leather sofa and matching armchair, plus a long walnut desk against one wall, with some files and a closed laptop on it. One wall was made up mostly of windows, though it was still too dark to see outside.

The most beautiful thing was the fireplace, which was made of rough-cut granite, with halved geodes interspersed in between the stone. The floor was hardwood, but there were wool rugs in muted tones here and there, and small tables with stacks of books on them, and sheets of paper with a masculine scrawl running from the very top to the very bottom of each page. Donovan was a writer?

I had just read the first paragraph on the topmost page when I heard the bathroom door open behind me. I whirled, quickly dropping the paper back down... and froze.

He was gloriously naked, except for a white towel wrapped around his waist. I knew it was a normal-sized towel, but it looked smaller on his massive form. His broad chest was covered with dark whorls of hair that led in a trail down to his groin. Tori and Nessa had dragged me to a Beefcake Boys dance show the year before, and the men in that had nowhere near the definition and allure of this gorgeous man.

I found myself crossing the floor to stand in front of him, one hand moving to touch the damp, quivering muscles of his abs.

"Sweetheart?" he groaned. "What are you doing?"

I didn't answer, just kept tracing the ridges along his sides, following the magnificent lines like a map that showed the way to hidden treasure.

"Hey." His hand caught mine, gently stopping it from continuing beneath the towel.

"Sorry," I muttered, sucking in a deep breath. His scent was heady and addictive, and I wanted it inside me. I wanted *him* inside me. But I wasn't Tori or Nessa. I wasn't the sister who demanded attention, or expected a man to fall at my feet, even if I was an omega.

Even if I was his true mate.

That thought was like a shock of cold water to my libido. I cleared my throat, holding out the phone. "Nicky wants to talk to you."

Donovan took it, then turned away and crossed to the windows to place the call. I couldn't stay in the room with him, not when he was only wearing a towel and talking to my brother. So I let myself explore the kitchen.

I moved slowly, wondering at the perfection of the space. It was at least as big as the living room, with countertops and cabinets for days. There was an enormous Sub-Zero French door refrigerator next to the larger of two sinks. Hand-labeled glass jars filled with dried herbs lined the windowsill above the deep, ceramic sink, with a small curtain decorated with cut lemons perched at the top.

The stove was a yellow-enameled Aga Mercury convection model, the same one I had put in my apartment, but in a better color. The walls were painted a pale buttery yellow, and the quartz countertops had small streaks of yellow and green in them. There was a long shelf with recipe books, and a collection of green Le Creuset cast-iron enamelware stacked below it. Glass-fronted shelves above the counters gave glimpses of crystal stemware and a collection of mismatched mugs, as well as hand-thrown pottery tableware in shades of green and blue by an artist I'd seen in Denver.

I knew my jaw had dropped, taking in all the details of the room, but I couldn't help it.

It was my dream kitchen. Everything about it was perfect. I opened the fridge—it was empty, except for some butter, an unopened container of cream, condiments, and a lonely glass dish that may have had some kind of pudding in it before it had dried up. The freezer was packed with frozen vegetables and fruits, raspberries mainly, though there were blocks of cheddar and gruyère tucked around the other packages as well. I wandered to one narrow door and opened it, taking in the pantry's organized dry ingredients.

Before I could think through what I was doing, I had rolled up the sleeves of my robe, gathered butter, flour, salt, sugar, baking powder, cream, and a bag of frozen raspberries, and had the oven pre-heating. The comfortable, routine dance of baking had always been where I found happiness.

"Do you mind if I watch?"

My happiness ebbed slightly. I shook my head in response, not looking away from the pan where I was melting the butter. Donovan entered the kitchen and leaned back against a counter, his arms crossed over his chest.

"You love to bake," he commented after a moment. I rummaged in a cabinet for a glass dish, pouring the butter into it before answering.

"I love to make things. Sew, weave, cook. But baking is a special kind of magic."

He didn't interrupt me, or try to fill the quiet. I measured out the flour, salt, sugar, and baking powder, whisking them together, before adding the cream and a tablespoonful of water. After a moment, I said, "The dry ingredients are boring, on their own. They don't taste good; they don't look like much. But without them, you can't make a cobbler."

"Raspberry cobbler?" Donovan's throaty growl was unexpected, and I peeked up. He looked ravenous, but his dark eyes were on me, not the mixing bowl. "You're making my second favorite dessert in the world."

"What's your favorite?"

"Cinnamon rolls with vanilla icing." I shot him what I hoped was a suspicious look. "It's true. Honestly, I'll eat anything with vanilla," he said with a grin. For a second, I thought he was trying to flirt, but he just shrugged when I frowned at him. "My mom used to tease me about it. I'd put vanilla on every single food or drink anyone gave me. I tried putting it on eggs once." I grinned back at him, and he smiled wryly. "It's the only thing I won't add it to."

"Unless you're making a vanilla custard," I mused aloud, pouring the sugared berries on top of the other ingredients and sliding the dish into the oven. "I didn't see any vanilla in the pantry..."

"Probably drank it all up," he murmured. When I scoffed, he stared back, unrepentant. "I put it in coffee. My dad used to as well."

I almost smiled. "Does your family live close by?"

A flicker of something—pain?—shadowed his eyes for a moment, then was gone. "No. My parents both work and live on cruise ships, believe it or not. They just celebrated their fortieth anniversary halfway across the Pacific."

"They live on cruise ships?" I laughed as I started washing up. He tsked and took the dish out of my hands, his own fingers sliding on mine. A burst of vanilla and cinnamon surrounded us, but neither one of us mentioned it.

"Yes. Believe it or not, Duchess Cruises is a phenomenal company to work for. Mom is the bursar on one of their larger ships, and Dad is an emcee. Rita actually worked as a lounge singer on board once. Those ships are gorgeous, and the crew have fantastic accommodations and benefits, unlike the larger cruise lines."

We finished the dishes in silence, and then, to my surprise, Donovan picked me up again, carrying me into the bathroom. He set me down, then went back into the kitchen for a stool. Gently sitting me on top of it, he began finger combing my hair.

"What are you doing?" I yawned halfway through my question.

In the mirror, his smile transformed his craggy, bearded face until it was infinitely beautiful. "Brushing your hair out while we wait for the cobbler." He picked up a brush and smoothed it down my almost-dry locks. "You have such beautiful hair. Like dark honey."

"I was thinking of cutting it," I murmured. "It's hard to take care of."

"Don't. I'll take care of it for you," he said quietly, gathering it up at my nape in one hand and sliding his fingers down the side of my neck with the other.

I shivered. "What do you mean?"

"I mean, I'll take care of it from now on." His fingernails scraped lightly over my collarbone, and goosebumps rose up on all my limbs. "I'll take care of you."

"But you said... you signed a contract."

"Your brother fired me."

"He can't do that!" I pulled away, incensed. "I'll tell him—" A large finger landed on my lips, silencing me.

"So sweet. You'd fight for me, wouldn't you? You'd find the strength to stand up to the world for me?"

I met his gaze in the mirror. "If-if I have to. Yes."

His dark eyes blazed. "You never will, baby girl. Protecting you is my job. Taking care of you. Giving you everything you need, making sure you're safe. It doesn't matter if it's my profession. It's my whole life, do you understand, sweetheart?"

I wasn't certain what he was saying. Was he... claiming me? "Y-Yes?"

"Yes, who?"

"Yes, D-D—" I held my breath for a moment, as a strong surge of eucalyptus and cedar rushed around us. Behind me,

Donovan canted his hips forward, and I felt his cock press against my back, between my shoulder blades.

"Don't be nervous, sweet girl. You can say it."

"W-what?" I whispered.

"I've been watching you for the past few weeks. I've seen the books you read. I heard you in the car, my perfect baby girl. I know what you want to call me. And I want it more than you can know. But I need you to say it." He pressed harder, pulling my hair gently so that my head tilted back, then let out a soft growl when I didn't speak.

Oh god, oh god, oh god. I was so turned on, I could feel the wetness seeping into the robe again. He knew... He knew what I wanted. And he didn't think I was perverted, or disgusting. At least, I hoped not. I closed my eyes tighter, hoping I wasn't about to make a terrible mistake.

"Yes...?"

"Yes, Daddy," I managed to whisper.

His growl instantly changed to a purr that traveled through my body like a tremor, changing everything it touched. "That's my good girl. My perfect girl." His thumb moved over my lips, tracing them, and I opened my mouth. "Open for Daddy."

To my shock, his thumb slipped over my tongue, before he gently grasped my cheek. With his thumb and forefinger, he carefully turned my face to one side, then leaned over to place his lips on my neck. I moaned as he nipped and lapped at the soft skin there, his teeth grazing my flesh. His beard rasped over my skin, the tiniest bit painful. I wanted more.

When he finally pulled back, I was breathing like I'd run a race. A cramp started up again in my core, and I groaned.

"You're going into a mating heat." He pulled his thumb out and traced my lips with it, the movement soothing me. "I know you're scared. But you don't need to be. I'm going to help you through it. I'm going to make you feel better."

I wanted to cry, from gratitude... and fear. "I'm scared," I admitted, my heart racing. The only heat I'd ever had had been terrifying, and ended with me in the hospital.

I saw understanding in his gaze. "You don't need to be afraid. I'm not going to hurt you. I'll never hurt you." His voice thrummed with honesty. "Look at my perfect girl," he said, moving his thumb back inside my mouth. He brought his other hand around and placed it like a collar around the front of my neck. "Suck Daddy's thumb, sweetheart. I need you to relax."

My eyelids fluttered closed as I obeyed, his light grip on my neck not enough to make my head spin, but feeling dizzy nonetheless. I sucked at his thumb, drawing the flavors of him inside me, wishing it were another part of him I was exploring. After a while, my heartbeat had settled, but a second pulse had started up in my clit. Every suck on his thumb was echoed below, and when he pulled it away, I whimpered.

"Shush, baby girl. I need to see all of you." He kept his hand on my neck, but used the other to open the front of the silky robe, taking in my flushed skin. "Look at those perfect, tight little nipples," he murmured softly, using his free hand to cup first one, then the other, rolling the beaded flesh in between his damp thumb and forefinger. "Like little raspberries, sweet and ripe."

He blew a stream of cool air onto them, and the wetness from my own spit made them tighten even farther. Using the hand around my neck, he lifted my chin. "Look at that. Look how small you are under my hand, baby girl. So little." He spanned one entire breast with his hand, squeezing rhythmically.

I felt a strange swirling feeling in my lower abdomen. Not a cramp, but something pleasurable and new.

"Spread your legs," he growled in my ear. "I need to see if you're getting wet for me."

Holding his gaze in the mirror, I obeyed, moving the robe out of the way and baring my mound, with its patch of honey-brown curls. He inhaled, drawing my scent into his lungs, and pressed against my back once more.

"Open your lips, sweetheart. Show me that pretty little pussy."

My eyes were wide now, and my chest was as red as my cheeks. I did what he asked, though I winced at the slick that gleamed on my thighs. I began to close my legs, but he tsked.

"Did I say to shut your legs?" He let go of my neck and moved away.

"I'm sorry," I began, but he wasn't leaving. He'd just moved around the stool and was kneeling on the floor in front of me, the towel knotted around his waist falling to the floor. From this angle, all I could see were his shoulders, head, and back. He had scars all over his bronzed skin, some that were round and shiny, raised above the rest. "Are those from bullets?" I gasped.

"The world is a dangerous place, little one. That's why I'll never let you be alone. Why you need to listen to me when I tell you to do something, okay? You be a good girl, and I'll take care of everything. Now, I need to concentrate on this sweet little cunt. I'm going to give you an orgasm, sweetheart. Maybe more than one."

When I started to protest, he wrapped his hands around my upper thighs and spread me so wide, it ached slightly. "I'm not asking, baby girl. I'm telling. I'm going to suck this little clit" —he swiped his tongue right over it, making me squeal—"and fuck this little virgin hole with my tongue." Lowering his head, he poked just the tip of his tongue into me. I had a feeling he meant to go on, but he groaned and went back, lapping and slurping, like he was drinking my slick. "Fucking delicious," he mumbled against my swollen lips. "Damnit, I could eat this pussy every day of my life."

I almost giggled, but then he moved his head back to my clit and began to suck and circle, nip and tease. The swirling sensation got stronger, and a matching wave of anxiety started up inside. This was what it always felt like, right before I didn't come.

"Your thoughts are distracting you, sweet girl," Donovan murmured. "That means I need to give you something else to think about. I'm going to put my finger inside you, okay? It's going to make you feel even better, when I curve it up toward your clit, like you're being rubbed on both sides. Have you ever done that?"

"No." I panted, feeling the anxiety begin to fade, and a curiosity begin.

"Do you want it?" He circled my clit a few more times, bringing the feeling back quickly, then paused. "Answer me."

"Yes." I thrust my hips up slightly, trying to get his tongue back where it had felt so good.

He stopped licking entirely. "Yes, who?"

My face in the mirror was bright red. I swallowed hard, then whispered, "Yes, Daddy."

"Say, 'Yes, Daddy, lick my pussy until I come all over your face.'"

I slammed my eyes shut, but he wouldn't start again until I said it.

Chapter 9

Donovan

Her sweet voice trembled as she obeyed. "Yes, Daddy, lick my pussy until I come all over your face."

I grinned into her slick-soaked core and got to work. I was going to Hell for this, and I didn't even care. Every time she called me Daddy, my cock jerked like she'd called him by name.

I hadn't ever been called Daddy before. I'd never even imagined it would turn me on like this, until a few weeks ago when I was watching Valentine read on the rooftop solarium at her apartment. She'd nodded off in her cushioned Adirondack chair, and the book—inside a fabric sleeve—had fallen to the ground. I'd picked it up, intending to mark the page for her, and discovered that my sweet little charge had been fascinated by a story titled *Daddy's Little Omega*. And then I'd gotten immersed, for a solid half hour, while she slept.

After only a few pages, I'd known why she had a cover to disguise it, and it wasn't just for the title. The paperback had been dogeared, the original cover torn, and the spine cracked in a half-dozen places. It had fallen open to one of those when I picked it up, to a scene where the main character was suckling gently on her lover's cock, using it as a comfort item. The book had referred to it as cock warming, a term I had never come across. I'd thoroughly researched it since then, as well as a host of other, related sexual kinks.

I hadn't been certain this type of play would really appeal to my charge. People read a lot of things, right? But she'd read this particular book until it was falling apart.

The mere thought of Valentine reading that kind of story—and enjoying it—had me so hard I'd been leaking in my pants, and aching for the rest of the day. I'd been shocked. After years of being uninterested in sex, it had taken up center stage in my fantasies.

But only sex with her.

Now she was calling me Daddy. *Begging* me to lick her. It was ridiculous. I would give up every possession I owned for one hour with my tongue in her pussy.

I plunged it in again, then moved back to her swollen clit, loving the way her hands threaded through my short hair as she struggled with the waves of pleasure she was feeling. It was all new to her, and I loved the idea that her first real climax would be from my mouth.

And my hands. With one hand still holding her thigh, I lifted the other to her wet entrance, angling my hand so my finger would crook upward, against the front wall. I'd seen this technique in a series of videos I'd watched over the past month, but I'd only gotten the first inch of my finger inside her when I realized there was going to be a problem.

"Um, Donovan?" she gritted out. "That's... just one finger?"

She sounded concerned. I was every bit as worried. I'd never imagined a woman could be this small. Tight, hot, and impossibly narrow.

I kept licking, working the tip of my finger up to the first knuckle into her, my mind buzzing with a combination of lust and concern. "It is, baby doll. Just relax, let me in. I'm going to make you feel so good." I renewed my licking, stroking as gently as I could with my fingertip until she relaxed, and I was able to push more of my thick forefinger inside.

She was so tight, I knew I wouldn't be fucking her anytime soon, heat or not. I'd have to stretch her, get her used to one finger, then two. Maybe use her toys—that was it.

Her next sound was half-whimper, half-shriek, as finally I was able to reach the spot inside that I'd been seeking. She cried out as I circled my tongue faster, a little harder, my finger inside mirroring the motion.

"Yes!" She exploded in a climax that had her pussy tightening so hard on my finger, it almost hurt. Her juices flooded out of her and all over my beard, soaking me in her cinnamon-sweet aroma.

I felt like I'd won every lottery in the world. Like I'd justified my existence on the earth. I'd given this perfect woman true pleasure. I hummed around her clit, gentling my motions for a moment until I realized... she was crying.

Instantly, I had her face in my hands, my eyes on her tear-filled ones. "Baby girl, did I hurt you? What's wrong?"

"I just... never..." She couldn't finish her sentence, but I understood.

"That really was your first one, wasn't it?" I asked, and she nodded as I gathered her up to my chest. I carried her to my bedroom as she sobbed, mumbling what sounded like *thank you*, as well as something about telling her sisters.

I rocked her until she fell asleep. Then I took the cobbler out of the oven, helped myself to a large serving, and carried a bottle of water into the bedroom.

I let myself think about what her brother had said on the

phone. How he'd threatened to cut my dick off if I hurt her, and then quietly asked me to see her through her heat, if it came.

"She's been on suppressants for five years. The only memory she has of a heat was her first experience, when she was attacked by a group of boys at school. Some of them had already revealed as alphas, and they used their barks to make her hold still while they... Well. That's why we forbid any alphas from barking. She goes almost catatonic when she hears it."

I fought the urge to tear down the door, go find those assholes, and rip out their spines. "I read the file, and Bobby gave me a few details. I need more information on the health concerns she's having, though. I can't keep her safe if I don't know everything. Why would her doctor prescribe sex?"

Nicholas Paxson sighed deeply. "At the end of December— not long after you took the job—she started having complications. Shortness of breath, heart palpitations, all signs that she's been on the suppressants too long."

"Tell me she's not still taking them." Had I seen her slip a pill in her mouth? My blood went cold.

"She's been on a much lower dose. Her doctor has been weaning her off the pills, and the ones she has left are only meant to be taken in an emergency. If her heat started around an unsuitable alpha..."

"I'm unsuitable, Mr. Paxson. You don't need to say it. I'll bring her ho—"

"No. I need to ask something else of you. I know it's not your job. The girls all say you're the best option." It sounded like he was chewing glass as he went on. "The other men call you—"

"Monk. I know." I cleared my throat. "I'm not one. You know what I mean. I just... I'm not celibate." I had a feeling

Paxson would have accessed my health records, so I didn't mention that I was clean.

"Good. That's good. I don't want to ask you to do something against your nature."

"Helping her would not be against my nature," I replied, my face flaming. "It's my job."

"Hell no. You can't be an employee if I'm going to ask this of you. I'll have to fire you."

"If you didn't, I'd have to quit," I agreed.

"I'll text Storm Halder now, and let him know. You'll get unemployment—"

I scoffed. "I may not be a billionaire, but I've got more than enough. I was about to retire anyway."

"Thank you. We need you to stay with her. Her heat may or may not even happen. It could take a week or more to fully set in, and she'll need... you."

He'd hung up the phone with a promise to hunt me down and slit my throat if I ever hurt his sister—a threat I welcomed. I stared down at her sleeping face, tucking a few damp tendrils of honey-brown hair behind one ear and wondering how an unworthy asshole like me had gotten so lucky as to have her. Even if it was only for a few short days.

At last, I curled up next to her, intending to nap for a few minutes.

"Donovan?" A small voice pulled me from the familiar nightmare—or memory, really—that had me in its claws. A vision of blood, and terror, and a woman begging me to stop.

And me, not stopping.

"What's wrong, Valentine?" I asked, looking around. She was hunched over, her back to me. The bedside clock said ten a.m., and I blinked at it for a second, stunned. I never slept this late, or this long.

And Valentine had been alone, awake.

"Baby—" I stopped as I heard a whirring sound. That's when I noticed that the bed was littered with the sex toys I'd purchased on our trip. "How long have you been up?" It must have been a lot longer than a few minutes; she'd unboxed everything, and the bed resembled...

She giggled. "It looks like a table at a sex worker's yard sale, doesn't it?"

"Pretty much."

Valentine twisted to peer at me, a sheet pulled around her flushed body. Sweat dampened the tendrils of hair around her face. She'd pulled her hair up into a knot of some kind, and when she turned, I could see she had a vibrator in each hand. One was a thick dildo with a simulated alpha knot. The other was a slimmer anal vibe with a flared base and a jewel at the end.

I was suddenly very, very hard. "What are you doing, baby?"

"I, um, well... I woke up and I had some water, and I ate some of the cobbler and then came back to bed with cramps, but you were fast asleep so I thought I could take care of it myself, since you showed me how, sort of, last night..." Her lower lip trembled as she stopped babbling. "But I can't figure it out."

A wave of sadness filled me, followed almost immediately by a dark rush of gratitude. Her fear and insecurity were the only reasons she couldn't come. I could fix that.

"I don't want you to figure it out, sweetheart," I said, taking the vibes out of her hands. "We need a few rules, okay? I'm going to be the one in charge. I don't want you to even try to have an orgasm without me; the only exception will be if I order you to touch yourself for me while I watch. Do you understand?"

"N-no," she admitted.

"What I mean is that I am in control in this room, this house, for this heat."

"I'm not sure it even *is* a heat," she interrupted. "From what my sister Lindyann says, omegas in heat can't even speak intelligibly. Or think."

"For this house, then. Under this roof." I waited for her to nod, then went on. "Your orgasms will all come from me. My tongue, my fingers, me holding the toys I bought for you. You won't use them or your own hands to climax. Can you promise me that?"

"Um, that's easy." I lifted an eyebrow. "Yes, I promise." I waited another moment, then frowned. Her cheeks went pink as she whispered, "I promise, Daddy."

"Good girl," I praised.

She squirmed on the bed. "I-I need to ask you something. Not about sex. Well, mostly." I could tell she was truly worried about something.

"Anything. I'll never lie to you, Valentine."

"Have you... The Daddy thing... Are you doing that for me? Or is it your thing? Have you done this with other women?" Her eyes were squeezed shut by the end of her outburst, and I sat up, pulling a sheet over my lap and around my waist before taking her hands in mine.

"Sweetheart, you don't need to be embarrassed. No. I have not ever wanted to have another woman call me Daddy. Not one ever has."

"Then... how?" she whispered. "How did you know?"

"I read one of your books."

"Which one?"

I grinned at her wide eyes. "*Daddy's Little Omega*. I read a few pages of yours, then bought my own copy on my e-reader."

"Oh." Her mouth stayed in a little circle as I went on.

"I liked it. The way he cared for her, and she gave him control. The gentleness of it. I looked into some of the other types of Daddy play as well." I took a breath, looking for the right way to say this. "I'll try anything you want, but—"

"I'm not into the age play thing," she interrupted. "And... I don't like the ones with the spanking."

I suppressed a relieved sigh. "Good to know. I wouldn't have been able to do that. I told you I'll never hurt you, and that was a promise." I winked. "Though I can come up with some punishments that don't hurt, if you're a bad girl."

She gulped audibly. "I won't need punishments."

"We'll see." I gripped her hands more firmly. "We need to talk about a few more things before this goes any further. I need to know what's not okay. What your limits are."

Her hands tightened. "I'm n-not good at t-talking about—" She broke off, taking a deep breath. "I'm unsure."

"Then you need to tell me if you don't like something. Or if you're worried, or scared. It's my job to notice, but sometimes, in the heat of the moment... I need to know you'll tell me."

She screwed up her nose. "Like a safe word?"

"If you like."

She shook her head. "That always seemed weird to me. I don't want..." She went on, grimly. "I don't *want* to be in charge. That's the part I liked most about that book. She didn't have to make the decisions."

"Then just say stop, okay? I'll stop and make sure you're all right."

She nodded. "Um, one thing." I knew what was coming. "No barking. Ever."

I knew why she said that, and a wave of buried rage threatened to consume me. Instead, I squeezed her hands gently. "I will never bark at you, Valentine. Not for anything." I shifted on the bed, and the sheet that had been draped around my waist fell away.

Her gaze dipped immediately to my cock, and I held still as she took it in. Her face went a little pale, and she swallowed hard. "Oh, holy shit."

I bit my lip to stop myself from smiling. My cock was big, but not as big as some alphas. My knot, on the other hand... I refocused on Valentine. "No cursing, sweetheart, or I really will have to come up with a punishment."

She apologized softly, her gaze still fixed on my rigid length. "Sorry, Daddy." Her scent had gone bitter, true fear lacing it.

That would never do.

"Have you ever held a cock before, sweetheart?"

No. She mouthed the word, but didn't even blink.

"Would you like to touch mine?" Supporting my weight on one side, I pushed my hips forward, giving her a better view.

"Um, I d-don't think, I don't think I'm going to b-be able to —" Her panicked voice disappeared in a squeak.

I laughed. "I'm not going to fuck you. I'm not going to do anything that scares you, or hurts you. Do you understand?" I kept my voice calm and gentle, but dropped one hand to my dick, holding it at the base so she could see it better. "Here's another rule. This cock belongs to you now. You can touch it anytime you like, in any way."

"Even with teeth?" For some reason, she giggled when I winced.

"If you need to. Anything you want to try, you can. It belongs to you now. Just like your orgasms belong to me. Got it?"

She nodded, took a steadying breath, then leaned forward. I

fell back onto my elbows, exposing myself to her completely. I'd never felt so powerless, helpless under her gaze. But I'd also never felt more attractive, as her eyes worshiped my body, her small hands tracing my muscles. I knew I wasn't handsome, but the way she looked at me made me think she hadn't figured that out yet.

After she'd touched me for what felt like an eternity, but had to be only a few minutes, she asked breathily, "Can I... Can I put it in my mouth?"

Fuck, yes. "I would love that."

I'd always been told Hell was hot. I hadn't known Hell was the exact temperature of my little virgin mate's mouth, too-gently sucking at my cock. I held still, every muscle tense, as she tentatively explored me, her tongue darting into the slit on the end, tasting my salty pre-cum before she hummed like she was at a wine tasting. She lapped at the sides, mapping the veins that stood out on the underside. Finally, she returned to the crown and sucked it gently into her mouth, moving just the tip of it into the perfect wet heat, her tongue swirling around it.

"You taste so good," she mumbled around the head. "Do you drink pineapple juice?"

What? I briefly laid one hand on her cheek, checking to see if her heat fever had returned. She was a little warm, but not terribly so.

"That's just my taste." My voice sounded like someone had taken a cheese grater to my vocal cords. I stared up at the ceiling, fighting the urge to move my hands from the sheet, to grab her head and thrust my cock into her mouth, spill my cum down her hot throat... "Oh, *fuck*," I groaned as the thought of it sent me over the edge. Even in the middle of my orgasm, I tried to pull away so she wouldn't choke, but she followed me, sucking and swallowing as fast as she could, like my cum was her favorite flavor.

"Yummmm," she said, coming off with a little pop of her lips. "Are you sure you don't drink pineapple juice? Because that was delicious. I'm gonna suck your dick every day—"

"*Your* dick," I reminded her.

She gave a Cheshire cat grin. "My dick. Like I said, I'm going to suck it and drink it down every morning for breakfast. And every night before I go to sleep. Maybe even at lunch." She went back to the head and started sucking again. It was too sensitive, and I winced, but she kept going.

I let her. It wasn't my dick, after all.

Chapter 10

Valentine

I had a feeling I was terrible at giving head. I also knew it didn't seem to matter one little bit. Donovan had gotten flustered at coming so fast, but it had done wonders for my fragile ego.

Donovan was everything I could have hoped for. He was confident and assertive, but the way he looked at me made me think deep down, he might need me as much as I needed him.

The way his stern face softened with something like awe as I touched and stroked him brought tears to my eyes. My sisters had told me Donovan hadn't had a lover in years. But I had a feeling no one had touched him at all for at least as long.

At least, not with love.

Could I love him? I had a feeling, if I was honest about it, the answer was yes. All it would take was a little more time, and a few more moments where he showed me the gentle, tender heart inside the Viking-sized exterior.

But I wasn't certain about him loving me. There was a lot of space between "my dick belongs to you" and "my heart belongs to you."

My pussy sure belonged to him. After I'd swallowed all his cum, he'd asked for his turn and spent the next hour with his tongue either on my clit or inside me, and his finger stretching me, driving me to one peak after another.

A part of me was dying to call my sisters and tell them it had finally happened. I'd had the Big O, as they called it. The kind where my whole body was consumed in fireworks, my legs went numb, I screamed myself hoarse, and my clit pulsed with a second heartbeat for ten minutes after.

After the first three, Donovan had started pulling his mouth away, and giving me permission to come right before he triggered the next one.

No, not permission. He had started *ordering* me to come on his tongue, using the filthiest language. I didn't think it was his words that made me tumble over the edge, but hearing them now seemed to set me up to climax a lot more quickly.

I hadn't taken any more pills, not that I would have had time. And not that I wanted to, now.

The mating heat that had been threatening the night before had now returned with a vengeance. All day, the cramps and low fevers were coming in waves, then retreating. But for some reason, they wouldn't settle. The mental haze kept clearing, replaced with the nagging feeling that something was missing.

Something was wrong, and I had no idea how to verbalize it.

The bed was comfortable and smelled great, but it wasn't right. The room had two large windows, and furniture everywhere. It didn't feel... safe.

But I knew I couldn't tell Donovan that. He was obsessed with keeping me safe. Even from his own dick.

Correction, *my* dick. I had to get the pronouns right, dang it. I had a dick now, and I needed to remember that. Donovan was letting me play with it again, and I gave it a soft suck, whispering, "That's my good dick."

I was still concerned about fitting it inside me. If one of his fingers had hurt going in, there was no way that monster was going to make it through. But he'd just chuckled every time I mentioned it, and kept promising he would never hurt me.

I was beginning to think he meant he was never going to fuck me.

As if it knew what I was thinking, his dick began to grow harder and thicker under my tongue, and Donovan sat up on his elbows. "You need more orgasms, baby girl?"

"I need... something else."

He was at my side immediately, feeling my brow. "Heat's coming on faster now. I'll go get some water and things."

"I need juice," I said, suddenly overwhelmed at the knowledge that if I didn't take more pills now, then it really was here. And I wouldn't be going into it with a safe, cocktail-sausage beta.

"Juice? What else?"

"I need some... different lights. Softer ones. I need apple juice and... lemonade. Oh god, I need *lemonade!*" Suddenly, it seemed vital that I have it.

Donovan was out of bed, pulling clothes out of his drawers, before I could even finish the request. "Can you get dressed? We can go get whatever you need."

"I can't. I need to fix the nest," I told him, fretting with the bedding. "And I don't have clothes."

"You can wear the dress—"

I hissed. "It smells like the turd."

Donovan frowned. "Yeah. I'll throw it away." He pulled on a pair of gray sweatpants and a black, form-fitting t-shirt. His dick—*my* dick—was visible through the fabric of the pants, and the shirt revealed every ridge of muscle.

"I need juice," I repeated, suddenly very thirsty. "And then I need my dick again. But I really, *really* need juice. Can't we get it delivered?"

He grinned. "It snowed all night. The Hummer is safe on the roads, but the lady who owns the grocery store, Maggie Barnes, is ninety-two and the nosiest lady ever to walk the earth. If she made it here in her beat-up truck, she'd stay for hours."

"How long would it take to get there and back?"

"Fifteen minutes."

"Go," I growled. "Get some real milk, eggs, and dark chocolate, if they have any."

"And vanilla?"

"All the vanilla."

He grabbed me and gave me a long, thorough kiss, rubbing his beard on my face and neck—scent-marking me—before pressing his phone into my hand. He set it to unlock with my fingerprint, then opened his contacts. "If you need anything, the grocery store is called Magpie's Nest. If you want to call your sisters, now is the time." He started a countdown timer at fifteen minutes. "You don't take one step out of this house, Valentine. Not one."

"I promise I won't."

He wasn't gone one minute before my first heat spike started. It was like my body wanted to punish me for letting him go without me. I crawled to the bedroom and nestled in the middle of the rumpled blankets, but the harsh light from the windows and the obvious lack of my alpha made the pain worse.

I dragged myself to the bathroom and thought about

crawling into the tub. My new almost-sister-in-law, Candy, had done that when she was alone during a heat spike. She'd told me afterward that she needed a small space, and that was all she had. But Donovan's shower had a huge half-wall of glass cinder blocks, and felt even more exposed than the bedroom.

So I sobbed my way to the only room I hadn't explored yet... and felt like Goldilocks. The room was almost empty, except for a lamp and a queen-sized mattress on the floor.

It was just right.

With a sudden burst of energy, I ran for the burrito blanket, fishing it out of the hamper along with Donovan's dirty clothes from the day before. Next, I grabbed all the blankets off the big bed, as well as the pillows, and used them to make edges of my nest. There was a chest with more quilts, which made everything softer. Then I plunked down the bag I'd refilled with the toys Donovan had bought for me, and fixed a few more things in the room that needed adjusting.

Finally, it was all perfect. Turning the lamp on the lowest setting, I shut the door. With the phone pressed to my chest, I rocked back and forth, watching the timer move toward zero as I did my breathing exercises. I had done lots of harder things than waiting for fifteen minutes, while ripples of what felt like hot pokers unraveling my intestines tore through me. I'd make it through this.

I had to.

Chapter 11

Donovan

"Valentine!" I shouted from the front porch as I unlocked the door. The light on the keypad wasn't blinking, so I knew no one had gone in or out, but my inner alpha nature had been raging since I'd climbed into the Hummer. The snow had been high, and I'd more or less offended every person in the small grocery store in my hurry to get my omega what she needed. But now I was back home.

My arms loaded with over-full grocery bags, I kicked the door shut behind me. The living room was a mess, with rugs moved, and the cushions on the sofa and chairs missing. "Valentine?"

There was no answer.

She had to be here somewhere. I raced to the bedroom to find the bed empty. More than empty—this room also looked like it had been ransacked, stripped down to the mattress, with my shelves open and empty. The bathroom door was open, and the half-emptied laundry basket lay on its side, clothing scattered all around.

That only left one room. I opened the door to the empty

bedroom and blinked. "Sweetheart?" I murmured. "What... How?"

The room had been transformed. The lamp had a sheet draped artfully over the shade, diffusing the light. She'd strewn more sheets over the table and had somehow pinned some to the walls, blue and white alternating colors, with intricate, matching fabric roses tacked between them. Had she folded the roses out of pillowcases? Amazed, I stepped inside.

A low hiss came from the mattress in the middle of the room, though it wasn't a mattress anymore. It was a nest, with raised edges created from what had to be pillows, covered with blankets. I saw all the sex toys I'd bought tucked into the bases of the pillows, evenly spaced around the oval interior.

Inside the center of the nest was an enormous, lumpy tortilla that smelled like cinnamon cookies fresh from the oven, and a rich, buttery sweetness. A smile crept over my face. "Little burrito?"

"Why is sex always about food?" she answered. "You're not a cheeseburger. I'm not a burrito." She sniffled.

Quietly, I put the juice on the small table, and the rest of the food in the bags next to it on the floor. "Of course you're not. Omega, may I enter your nest?"

"Yes, please," she whispered, poking her flushed face out. My heart melted at her next words. "I didn't use any of the toys. Or my fingers. But it was hard."

"You were such a good girl. Do you need me to come in and help you?"

"I need..." She dropped her gaze, shy.

"You don't need to tell me. I know what you need, baby." I crawled over the sturdy sofa pillows that were lined up to make the edge, making sure not to knock any over. The purple vibrator she'd tried to use the night before was next to my hand, so I picked it up. Gently, delicately, I lifted the burrito blanket away from Valentine's shoulders, folding it to one side.

"First things first, I'm going to help you learn how to use this yourself." When she frowned, I tsked. "I'm in control of your orgasms, remember? I want you to learn how to come in whatever way I ask. And I may ask you to use this on yourself while I'm fucking that pretty mouth. I may want to come down your throat at the same time you're coming."

Her breaths were little pants now, and she nodded. I held the end of the vibe to her wet entrance and clicked it onto the lowest setting, causing her to whimper as I moved it around. "We'll practice coming at the same time with my mouth on your clit, too. That way I can taste you when you squirt all over my beard at the same time I come inside your little mouth." She had her eyes closed now as I moved the vibe along her slit, letting the small protrusions at the base make contact with the sides of her clit.

She began to shake and gasp as her orgasm approached, muttering my name, and Daddy, every so often.

"Come now, baby. Be a good girl and come for Daddy."

"Ah!" She tumbled into an instant climax, and I set her hip back down, turning her over and lifting her so she was on her hands and knees. Soon, I was going to train her to come on command from all sorts of things. I'd read enough to know that omegas—especially ones in heat—were susceptible to an alpha's suggestion, not just his bark. I couldn't wait to see if I could wring orgasms from her by playing with her nipples.

I grabbed the dildo that had a knot at the base, simulating an alpha. Well, not an alpha like me, but it had a slightly malleable knot, and I knew her body would need that extra pressure inside soon. "Give me your hand, baby." She rested her weight on her chest and obeyed. I wrapped her fingers around the wide base of the toy and pressed the narrow head slightly inside.

"So big," she murmured. I wanted to cry a little. The dildo was only about half as wide as my own cock. I pressed another inch in, working it from side to side, wiggling it until it was fully sheathed in her swollen passage. I crouched over her for a moment, kissing her shoulder and the side of her face.

"Hold it inside you, Valentine. Can you do that for me?"

Her bleary eyes met mine as she twisted to meet my gaze. "Daddy?"

"I'm going to lick you from behind now, sweetheart," I told her. "Then I'm going to show you something new."

"Something... Your knot?"

"No, baby," I muttered, knowing that was the one thing she'd beg for that I couldn't give her. I'd sworn never to do that again. But I'd make sure she didn't miss it. "I'm going to make you come in a new way." I wrapped my hands around her hips, pulling her toward me and kneeling so that her ass was directly in front of me. "Keep the toy all the way inside, sweetheart, and let me make you feel good."

When my tongue swiped over the tight center of her perfect ass, she let out a cry of shock. I waited, my tongue unmoving, to hear if she would ask me to stop, but all she said was a small, shocked, "Daddy!"

"Be a good girl now, okay, baby? Let Daddy explore."

She made a whimpering sound, and I went back to licking and tonguing her, relishing the shocked cries of pleasure she gave at the sensation of my tongue on her ass, stopping only to praise her or give her directions to thrust the dildo a little deeper inside.

Soon, the flared knot was all that was still outside of her channel. "Can you fit any more inside, baby?" I asked, after giving her ass one more thorough lick.

"No," she moaned, obviously frustrated. "Help me?"

"Of course, thank you for asking. Such a sweet girl." I grabbed some pillows to help her stay in position. "Keep your hips up. I'm going to work this knot inside you now. Let out a deep breath."

She did as I instructed, and I praised her wordlessly as I began to thrust the length of silicone into her, her cunt making wet sounds as the slightly more malleable knot met her outer lips.

She needed to relax to get the knot inside. I set my tongue back to work on her ass, pressing it into her slightly, then withdrawing it and pushing the knot inside her pussy, a fraction more each time. "Relax, baby. Daddy wants to see your little pussy spread out on the toy, and stick his tongue in this tight little ass. As soon as you take it all inside, I'm going to make you come all over it."

The dark, depraved part of me that wanted nothing more than to fuck her into next week, knot her until she was mewling and weeping on my girth, was rising too close to the surface. I pushed it down, reminding myself I was too old, too big, and too rough for a princess like her.

She shuddered, relaxing as I flicked my tongue over her ass, and the knot slid into her pussy. "What a perfect girl you are," I said, reaching around to her clit and working it. It felt almost distended, with the false knot pushing on the wall right behind it, and it took only a moment to have her on the edge. "Are you ready to come?" She nodded furiously, her face still pressed to the mattress, her hair spilling out around her. I leaned down and whispered the words right by her ear, circling her clit almost too gently as I did. "Come now, sweetheart."

Her shouts were so loud, the room rang with them, but when she finished shuddering, her tear-filled eyes met mine. "I need you, Donovan. I need you inside me. I need your cum."

"You're all filled up, Valentine. You have the knot toy inside," I murmured, wondering how I was going to explain that I was not ever going to put my knot in her little cunt.

"*Please.* I need your knot."

"I'm not doing that. I told you that."

"It's mine; it's *my* dick," she said, her voice trembling. "You said it was. I want it inside me."

"Okay, baby. How about sucking on it again?" I moved my hips closer to her face, but she shook her head stubbornly. I swallowed hard. She was an omega in her nest, and telling her no went against everything my instincts were driving me to do. "I can't, baby. Please know this. I want to. But I can't."

"Not yet?" she whispered.

Sure. "Not yet," I agreed, hating the lie. I was almost certain I could fuck her little cunt without slipping into a rut and knotting her.

But almost wasn't good enough.

Her lower lip jutted out adorably. "Then put it there." She pointed to her...

"Your bottom?" I blinked. "Baby, I can't..."

"Not all of you," she said, blushing furiously. "Just the tip."

I found myself grinning. I'd read that omegas loved having their alphas' cum all over them. And inside them. Maybe I couldn't come inside her pussy, but... "I think my good girl is naughtier than anyone knows."

"You're the one who licked it," she muttered, wriggling her hips up in the air.

"It tasted like your slick. I would eat your tiny ass every day." I grabbed a small bottle of lube from where she'd tucked it between two pillows, and rubbed some on the head and first few inches of my rigid cock.

Her cunt was stretched wide around the false knot, and my inner alpha wanted nothing more than to pull it out and replace it with the real thing. But I ignored the urge, moving back to her ass. "You want me to put a little bit of my cock in here?" I asked, spreading a little lube around her hole and using a finger to press inside. She whimpered, and I moved more slowly, inserting one, then two fingers, noticing how her pussy clenched around the knotted toy as I stretched her gently.

"Now, I want you to rub two fingers on your clit, okay, my perfect girl? You rub a little circle while I put just the head inside you." She obeyed, and I put extra lube on, pressing the thick head of my dick up to her tight opening. "It's going to feel so full, with that toy inside you. Don't worry, though. I won't do anything that hurts you. Remember—just say stop if you want me to stop." She nodded, and I exhaled, praying for control.

The feeling of her was incredible, and I could have come the instant my head breached the tight ring of muscle. But I managed to keep from embarrassing myself. I wanted to come when she did.

"Oh, baby, you're so spread out back here. Your pussy splayed out around that toy, and your little hole taking the head of my cock. Can you take a little more?"

"Yes, Daddy."

Fuck. I almost came again, hearing her call me that. "Daddy's going to push a little more of his cock into you. Let me know if it hurts." I groaned as she pushed back, as if she were trying to work more of me into her. But I was too thick for her to take much. I fucked her with the first inch or two, listening to make sure her cries were pleasure, and not pain.

"Please, *more*," she begged.

"Okay, princess," I managed to say through gritted teeth. "I need you to come, baby. Are you close?"

"Yes."

"Good girl. Now come on your little fingers, and I'll fill up this tight ass—*fuck!*"

She pushed her hips back hard, taking more of me—almost all of me—inside her hot channel. She clenched hard around me, her own climax barreling through her, as she forced me to fill her, and just like that, I was hurtling over the edge. I grabbed my knot, which was swelling to its full size—outside of her, thank god—to keep from accidentally losing control and pushing it inside.

I came for what felt like hours, my grip on my knot firm, even if my mind was hazing with the need to bury it in her. When my balls were finally empty and my cock beginning to soften, I pulled out slowly, carefully, though my knot was still close to fully engorged. Valentine collapsed to the mattress below, her shoulders shaking.

Oh fuck. Was she crying? A wave of dread poured through me and I got to my feet, ready to pick her up, rush her to the hospital if necessary. How had I hurt her?

"Sweetheart, talk to me. Look at me. What's wrong?" I held my breath, waiting for her answer. But it came as she turned over, her arms flopping to her sides on the mattress.

She was giggling, her face creased in a huge smile. "I'm fine. I'm more than fine. Now all I need is your..." Her voice trailed off as her gaze fell to my groin, and something close to horror replaced her amusement.

Chapter 12

Valentine

N
o. *Not gonna happen*, I thought for the hundredth time. *Not that knot.*

I was huddled on the bathroom floor, door locked, the sink running full blast, with Donovan's phone pressed as close to my face as I could get it.

"I don't know what to do," I whispered into the receiver. I'd called Nessa, and she'd immediately added Tori to the call, though I got the feeling they were in separate rooms.

"Of course you don't. You're a virgin."

"She *was* one," Tori broke in. "You said you built a nest. Hey, why aren't you in it? Doesn't a heat last, like, a few days at least?"

"I don't *know*. I told you Dr. G doesn't have any idea about what my heats will be like." They both made consoling noises. "We were fucking for a while, but I didn't have any problem leaving when I saw my death before me." I moaned. "I'm going to be a virgin forever. It's the only solution."

"Wait, what? What death?"

"His knot, Tori. His freaking *knot*." I cursed softly. "If that had accidentally slipped inside my butt when he came, I'd need to use a bedpan for the rest of my life."

The line went silent.

"Wait. You mean to tell us..." Tori made a weird sound, like she was choking. "He fucked your ass? But not your..." Both of them cackled for a while.

I almost hung up, until Nessa said, "I'm so jealous I could die. This is the stuff of legends. What was it like? On a scale from cold McDonald's to wagyu tartare—"

"He's Wagyu, A5." Doing what my sisters and I always did after a hot date, I gave them a quick rundown—though until this week, it had always been them giving the details of their sexcapades, and me listening. Over their oohs and ahs, I whispered, "The kinkiest part of all is he read my favorite book. And he's into it."

Tori snorted. "Wait, he dresses up like a vampire with glitter—"

Nessa and I both hissed her to silence. "That was my favorite book for five minutes in middle school. No, Tori. I mean, *Daddy's Little Omega.*"

The silence that followed was almost reverent.

Nessa murmured, "Does he... Oh god. Does he do that thing where he refers to himself in the third person? Calls himself...?"

Tori was whispering, "Oh please, oh please, oh please."

I sniggered. "You mean, does he say things like, 'Be a good girl for Daddy, and let Daddy put in another finger?'"

They both gasped.

"And 'You're taking it so well. Daddy's so proud?'" I waited for them to stop screeching. "Remember the cock warming scenes?" I purred. "He says it's not his dick. It's *mine.*"

Nessa shrieked. "No one in the world deserves a Daddy more than you, Valentine! But you know I'm going to live vicariously from now on, and if you don't share all the details..."

"Of course I will," I promised, though I wasn't certain I would tell them everything.

Tori hmphed. "So what's the emergency, babe? Why aren't you in there letting Daddy bounce you on his peen pony?"

"His knot is not ever going to fit," I explained. "I'm not kidding. I mean, his dick is girthy as heck, but doable."

"Soda can?"

"Almost."

"I hate you more now."

"Well, I thought the knot would be, like... in proportion. But it's a monster. Like, when he came—"

"In your ass," Nessa supplied.

"While you had a knotted dildo stuffed in your hoochie," Tori added.

I took a deep breath, praying for patience. "I'm so glad you were both paying attention. Now, please let me finish. As I was saying, his knot after he came was still outside me, but it had swollen up and... I'm not exaggerating, it's like a quadruple-meat cheeseburger. It will never, ever fit in my bun." I thought for a second. "Possibly not in *anyone's* bun."

Nessa sighed. "Listen, I'm looking up alpha-omega compatibility online in the American ABO Medical Journal right now. There has never been one documented case of an omega not being able to take an alpha's knot."

"Because they never saw Donovan."

"You know, anything is possible with enough lube." I shuddered when she tacked on, "Almost."

"Go take a picture of it," Tori suggested. "We can brainstorm once we see what we're working with."

"Pervert. I'm not going to go back out there and ask him to pose for a crotch shot to show my sisters!" I heard Donovan clear his throat outside the door, and slapped a hand over my face. "Oh no. He heard me."

Nessa's voice was gentle. "Listen. The man is your true mate. You said he promised never to hurt you. He didn't knot you yet—and he has to know what a monster he's carrying around. Maybe he's just as nervous about it as you?"

Tori swore. "You know Rufus was always giving him shit about not having any lovers, calling him a monk. Maybe Donovan wasn't *choosing* not to have sex. Maybe..." Her voice trailed off.

My heart lurched as I heard the front door of the cabin open and close. "Gotta run. I'll let you know how it goes." I wrapped the robe around me again and hurried to the front door.

Donovan wasn't getting into the car to leave, though. He was carrying firewood inside. I opened the door for him. He muttered his thanks, but wouldn't meet my eyes. He laid the fire, lit it, and only after it was blazing cheerily did he break the awkward silence.

"That was a long shower. How are your sisters?"

"They're, um, fine," I replied, tucking my toes under me on the sofa and staring at the flames. "I'm sorry I ran off."

"It was just a false heat spike then?"

"No, um, I'm pretty sure it was real," I squeaked. "But... I'd taken a couple of pills earlier today, so—" Before I could finish my sentence, he was up and leaving the room. "Donovan?" I called.

When he returned with my purse, he thrust it at me. "Get them out."

"W-what?"

He sat on the sofa beside me. "I'll go through your purse if I have to, but I don't want you to be angry with me. Get the pills out, and give them to me."

"W-why?" I asked, though I was already opening my clutch and handing him the small orange bottle.

"Your brother told me you were supposed to be off these now. That they were only for an emergency, if you started a heat in public. Or you felt unsafe."

"Yes?" I was so confused.

"So tell me, Valentine. Do you feel unsafe with me? Because if you do, I'm taking you back home now."

"No!"

"Do you feel like you can trust me?"

"Of course," I said, but my gaze dropped to his groin.

Disappointment and what might have been pain flashed across his face. "I've already promised not to hurt you. You need to believe me, sweetheart. I may not be good enough for you—hell, I *know* I'm not—but I couldn't live with myself if I thought you fear me."

"I fear everything," I admitted. "I'm a mess. I always have been."

He scowled. "Sweetheart, you're the finest woman I have ever met. You're generous and kind, quiet and unassuming. You are fiercely protective of the ones you love, and you speak up for the underdog. When I tell you I am unworthy, it is because no man could ever deserve your love."

I blinked, not sure how to respond. "But I'm awkward, and scared, and nothing like my sisters."

He laughed. "You're more like them than you let anyone see." He sighed, pouring the pills from one hand to the next. "Your family is what the rest of the world strives for. To have that many people who love you, who would fight the world for you. Who would do anything to protect you, doing whatever it takes to keep you alive, and whole, and healthy." He met my eyes and held up his hand. "Trust me, sweetheart."

And then he threw the pills in the fire.

I jumped up, lunging toward the fireplace. "*Fuck!*"

Donovan jumped up at the same time, pulling me down and onto his lap. "What did I tell you about using that sort of language?"

"You just threw my medicine away!" I ground my teeth together when he just lifted an eyebrow.

"It was bad for you. It was affecting your heart. Your brother told me you were supposed to stop taking it. That these were only for emergencies."

"And what if I have an emergency?" I laughed hysterically. "What if I have an alpha mate with a knot so big, it will rip me wide open? What if I'm scared to go into heat because I know I may not survive it?"

He held my chin in one massive hand and forced me to look into his face. What I saw there devastated me. His expression was... hopeless. "I'll only tell you one more time. I. Will. Never. Hurt. You."

"I'm so sorry, Donovan," I choked out. "I know that."

"You don't. But you will."

He adjusted me on his lap so that we were both facing the fire, and wrapped one arm around me, securing me in place. His other hand moved through my hair, gently untangling strands as he spoke so quietly, I had to strain to hear.

Chapter 13

Donovan

I t was one of the hardest things to do, telling the story I knew my little mate needed to hear. But she had to know. "This house was my home. I was born in the main bedroom."

She gasped. "Here? In this house? You've lived here all your life?"

"Not quite. I bought it and had it remodeled after my parents went to work for Duchess Cruises. My sister redecorated it for me. Rita and I shared the room your nest is in. It's a good thing she moved out for college, since that was about the time I hit puberty. She would not have wanted to share a room with a young, idiotic, fifteen-year-old alpha."

I allowed myself to remember how excited, how happy I'd been, to be like my dad. My parents had been thrilled. Alphas were larger and sometimes more aggressive, sure. But they also made phenomenal leaders and were respected.

"Dad was so happy. He helped me deal with all the new... energy surging through me by giving me more chores than any teen boys my age would normally do. I chopped firewood for the entire town and carried it from house to house, up the mountain road, in an old wheelbarrow. He said it was character building."

She giggled. I stroked her face, loving the feel of her soft skin. Wishing I didn't have to share the next part.

"Her name was Louella. She lived at the top of Aspenvale Peak with her parents, and when I met her, she invited me inside her folks' home. Louella was twenty-four, a beta, and had a reputation around town. She was pretty, I guess. Small-boned. She'd never bothered to talk to me, but when I took that load of firewood up her hill that spring—no shirt on, of course, because I was a cocky young shit—she must have changed her mind.

"Her parents were away for the month, and... I was over-whelmed. Literally. I was fifteen, and when she invited me in, and stripped off her dress—" I patted Valentine's hair sooth-ingly as she let out a soft growl. "Anyway. She knew what she was doing, or at least I thought that. I sure as hell didn't. She worked me up, teasing me, for hours. Wouldn't let me come, but rode my dick again and again. Said she wanted to try a knot. I told her Dad had warned me not to do that with a beta, that it could be dangerous. But she had a bottle of some perfume she'd ordered, Heat Effects."

"Oh no," Valentine whispered. "They took that off the market after a month! They banned it for causing... *Oh no.*"

"I learned later that it was the reason for my sudden rut. My violence." I pressed a kiss against her hair. "I wasn't anything special. Just an alpha with almost no sense, and even less control. The perfume and her aggression combined trig-gered my rut, my first one. I fell into the haze, and only came back to myself when I smelled blood.

"She was screaming underneath me. I had knotted her, and..." I had to stop talking to swallow the lump in my throat.

"She was a beta, but covered in omega pheromones," Valentine whispered, turning on my lap and pressing my head to her shoulder. I felt dampness there, and suddenly realized I was crying. "It wasn't your fault."

"It was." My voice was choked with tears. "By the time the ambulance arrived, I had managed to take it out."

"Did she..."

"She lived," I rasped. "Had to have a transfusion. Dad paid for her hospital stay. She tried to sue my family for more, but since I was underage, and she admitted she'd invited me in and asked for my knot..." I pressed my hand to my mouth, holding my breath.

"Oh, Donovan," Valentine whispered, then exhaled, her voice rumbling.

No. Purring. She held me close and purred as I mourned my own innocence, lost all those years ago. My parents had been so disappointed in me. I'd left home, enlisted in the army, served a tour overseas, returning with my first scars and a handful of ribbons and medals.

"My parents forgave me. But I never could." Slowly, one breath at a time, I began to pull myself back to the present. "After I left the army, I got a private job working to protect diplomats in volatile countries. I did a couple of years as a body-guard for that big K-Pop band." I named them, and she gasped. "Yeah, more than a few of my scars are from fans of theirs trying to take me out to get to them." I told happier stories from the years in between, and when I finally had my emotions under control, I sighed.

"I'm telling you all this because I need you to know that when I make a promise, I keep it. I slept with a few women, ten years after Louella. Two were sex workers, and I made them tie me down so I couldn't... hurt them. I didn't, but I didn't enjoy the experiences either. You know how you said you never knew what a decent orgasm felt like?" She nodded. "I was the same, believe it or not. For a long, long time, I didn't feel sexual attraction for anyone. Or at all, really. I only jerked off a couple of times a year, if that."

"What... When did that change?"

I grinned at her pink face. "About a month ago, when I showed up at a certain apartment in Denver and escorted the most beautiful, kind woman I'd ever met to a volunteer job as a sitter for poor infants." I kissed her lips gently, then her cheeks and eyelids, tasting her tears. My compassionate, sweet omega. "I see you, you know? You quietly make everyone else's dreams come true, but never ask for your own." She made a soft sound, and I kissed her again. "I saw you holding those babies, and wanted nothing more than to give you your own. You want babies, don't you?"

"Yes," she admitted.

"Then the pills had to go."

She blinked. "But... wait."

"I said I wouldn't knot you, sweetheart. I made a vow, and I'm sorry if it hurts your omega nature to hear it, but I won't."

I smoothed her damp hair back from her face, my heart so full of love for her, it ached. "I can't give you my knot. But I'll give you my heart... and as many babies as you want."

Chapter 14

Valentine

I was so confused. Happily confused, though.

"Your heart? Your—*our* babies? But, why?"

It was everything I'd ever dreamed, and as he smiled at me, I wondered if I was caught in a heat dream. "Why, baby girl? If you haven't figured it out by now, I love you."

I blinked. My tongue felt like lead. My heart was racing so fast, I was worried I might pass out. But the love and lust in Donovan's eyes gave me the strength to speak. I skipped over the love part—I was in no way ready to address that—and went to the biological impossibility of what he'd said.

"But don't you have to knot me—I mean, knot an omega to get her pregnant?"

He shook his head, a wicked smile beginning to curl over his face. "No. It's more effective that way. Easier. You're about ten times more likely to get pregnant from knotting, but that just means we'll have to fuck ten times more often." His hands dropped to my abdomen, opening the robe to touch my skin. "That won't be any problem. I'll fill you so full of my cum, there won't be any other option."

My pussy clenched, totally on board with that idea. "But... we're true mates. Don't you want to... claim me?" I'd read more than enough alpha-omega smut to know the mate bond happened when the alpha was knotted inside. "We can't bond —*ahh!*"

He had me in his arms, carrying me toward the nest, before I could finish. "Don't doubt me, sweetheart. I'll find a way to give you everything you need."

For a moment, I resisted, but then some inner part of me relaxed. This was my bodyguard. My protector. My true mate. He didn't just want me.

He loved me.

A new wave of prickly pains in my abdomen started again. But this time, I had a deep suspicion they wouldn't stop. Not until my heat—my real, full-length first heat—was over.

"Okay, Daddy," I sighed against his neck as he carried me back into the nesting room. "I trust you."

Donovan was the perfect alpha. He put me back in my nest, then ran to take the world's quickest shower. When he came back, he'd gathered up all the supplies we might need—food, drinks, stacks of towels, lube, and the rest of the sex toys I hadn't used in the nest in my omega heat haze.

Mostly, it was just stuff like anal beads and nipple clamps, but he'd also grabbed the Pussy Pounder 4.0 box. I watched him pull the remote control out and set it on the table, but then he hummed, reaching back into the box. There was another section in the bottom, and when he opened it, he let out a chuckle of satisfaction.

"What is it?" I asked, unwrapping my robe and placing it over one of the pillows. My nest was slightly messy, and my inner omega was waking up now, making sure I fixed it all before the next wave washed over me.

"Did you ever get a prize in the bottom of a cereal box?"

"No, but I heard about that from the old days. That was really a thing?"

He let out a mock growl. "Yes, little girl, back in the dark ages when I was a child, there were dinosaurs and steam engines and prizes in the cereal boxes." He opened the smaller package and pulled out a lavender silicone ring. It had bumps on it and a hole just the right size for a—

"Is that a beta knot?" I giggled. My sisters had told me about their beta friends who wore the false knots for fun. Though they'd agreed it probably wasn't anything like a real one, not that they'd ever dated any alphas.

"That's exactly right, princess," he said, shucking off his gray sweatpants. He spat in his hand and rubbed it on the inner edge of the ring, then slid it down his dick until it sat at the top of his real knot. Right now, the fake knot was about the same size as his. But I knew when he was coming inside me, it would be dwarfed by him.

"Now, what would you like to play with first?" He held up the remote, the nipple clamps, and the anal beads.

"Whichever gives me the most 'orgams,'" I teased.

"The Pussy Pounder 4.0 it is," he said, dropping everything but the remote with a wicked smile.

Chapter 15

Donovan

After I tried out the Pussy Pounder 4.0 on Valentine, we more or less played in the nest for the best part of an hour. There wasn't any real fucking going on, but laughter, conversation, and experimenting with some of the toys I'd bought her. My little mate had confided that the bag of toys was her favorite birthday present. I'd confided that I'd only ever read about a few of these things on the internet. We both researched what we could on my phone and decided what order to try the rest of the toys in.

It felt more honest, now that Valentine knew I wasn't all that much more experienced than she was in the bedroom. I knew she was only twenty-one, but that didn't seem to matter now.

Only that we were here, together. Made for one another.

"I know you like it that no other man has touched my pussy," she said, lying back in the center of the nest, opening her legs so I could see her wet core. "You like it that I'm your baby girl, and no one else's."

I nodded as she lifted her breasts toward me, rolling her

nipples in between her fingers. She was flushing red again, her heat overtaking her. I nudged her legs apart a bit wider and sucked in a deep breath of warm cinnamon and rich vanilla, my mouth watering.

"But I'm tired of being a virgin. I want you to fuck me."

"What did I say about cursing, baby girl?" I teased, grasping her thighs and opening them as wide as I could. "That's too many times. I'm going to have to punish you now."

"How can you—" she began, but I already had one hand pinching her clit, and the other plunged inside her, crooking upward.

In three quick thrusts, I ordered her, "Come now, baby girl. Come on Daddy's fingers." She obeyed perfectly, her legs shaking, small tits jiggling. I finger fucked her a bit more roughly as she climaxed, not letting the sensations end. While she was still crying out from her first orgasm, I rubbed quick circles around her swollen clit, then added another finger to her wet pussy, demanding, "Come. Come again, right now."

I'd only been training her to come for me for a day, but her body knew who it belonged to. She came again, whining the whole time. I set my mouth to her and wrung another three orgasms from her in quick succession, using my tongue and even my teeth to send her over the edge each time.

"No more, Daddy, please," she begged, tears streaming from her eyes. "I'll be good. I need... I need *you*." She began babbling as I licked her softly, then moved away, stroking her hair.

"You do want to be my good girl, don't you?" Her eyes were glassy, and I knew she would never be more ready for my cock. I made sure the false knot was still in place—my cock hadn't gone even slightly soft—and gently spread her out on the mattress. "You tell me if it hurts," I ordered. "Tell me to stop."

"Don't stop," she gasped, circling her hips as I set the tip of my cock to her opening. I pushed in gently, just the head, stopping to give her a moment to adjust.

She didn't want it. "More!"

I slipped in the tiniest bit more, feeling the resistance all around. The toys we'd used had helped somewhat, and she'd been able to take two fingers without discomfort, but I was still concerned.

"Does it hurt, baby?" I asked.

"N-no," she said, obviously lying.

Fuck. I started to pull out, and she gave a little grunt of anger, reaching up for my hips. She thrust upward, a small cry falling from her lips as she impaled herself on me, stopping only when her entrance met the plastic knot.

"Val—" I began, then bit my lip, hard, as she moaned. I levered away slightly, looking down as my cock slid out, the slightest trace of blood on the base. But so much more of it was slick, evidence of her desire.

"So *good.*" She chewed at her lip, mischief in her gorgeous eyes. She squeezed around my cock, milking me. "Fuck me hard, Daddy. Please? As hard as you can."

"Oh, you are a naughty girl." I pried her hands off my hips, gathering her wrists and pressing them to the bed. "You don't move those, or I'll force ten more orgasms out of you, do you hear me?"

She nodded, her eyes wide and excited. I wasn't sure if that nod meant she'd hold still, or if she was angling for punishment, but it didn't matter. I was already fucking her, sliding into her tight heat, pistoning harder than I should have for a virgin.

Her cries of pleasure filled the room. I couldn't focus; it was all I could do to fend off my own climax as she tightened around me, swelling again. The sex I'd had all those years ago had been *nothing* like this.

No other woman was anything like her.

107

I fucked harder, sensing that she was reaching another orgasm. From the way her legs were jolting, and her arms shaking, this one would be the one.

Still thrusting, I leaned down and scraped my teeth over the soft skin between her neck and her shoulder. "This is where I'm going to mark you, princess. When I knot you, I'm going to bite down here."

Her pussy clenched hard around me. "Will it hurt?"

"Only for a second. But it's a good hurt. And then I want you to bite me back. I want to feel those tiny teeth in me—"

Before I could finish, she'd already darted up and bitten my pectoral, hard. I hissed in a breath.

The pain was... wonderful. The kind of hurt that only added to the pleasure. She drew back, a shy smile on her face. I couldn't wait another second to claim her.

"Relax, baby, open for me," I demanded, staring in wonder at her blood-stained lips. "Now, *come!*" She was already spasming beneath me, around me, when I wrapped a hand around my own knot and pushed the slick-soaked beta knot inside her.

Her body closed down around it, as if it were mine, and I only felt a moment of sadness before I leaned over again and bit down carefully, feeling the heat of her blood in my mouth just as my cum began to fill her. My knot swelled up to its full girth under my hand, and I squeezed it as hard as I could, keeping control.

"That was amazing," she breathed. "Did it..." Our eyes met, and I saw my own concerns and hopes reflected in hers. "Can you feel me?"

"I don't know," I answered truthfully. "Shhh."

I closed my eyes, centering myself. I had so many emotions rocking me, it felt like a storm at sea. But were they mine, or hers... or both of ours? I recognized my underlying concerns that what I could give her wouldn't be enough. I felt a wash of relief, but I wasn't certain where it came from. Then love, a wave of undeniable love swept through me. That had to be mine, but there was so much of it, I couldn't tell.

For a moment, I felt insecure, as an alpha and a lover. I hadn't given her what omegas needed. Hell, I didn't even know if I'd claimed her. I knew I'd promised her I'd find a way, but without my knot inside her, it might not even be possible.

A peculiar feeling, like champagne bubbles, or indigestion, began inside me. I heard a snort, and my eyes snapped open. Valentine's gaze was locked on my knot, where my hand was still squeezing.

"What?" I asked.

She burst into giggles. "I'm sorry, it's just... you were squeezing it like a gas pump. And I could feel your cum still squirting every time you squeezed, and it was just funny." She bit her lip, trying to look serious. The champagne bubbles filled me up entirely.

"It's you," I breathed, holding a hand to my chest, feeling a fierce surge of joy. I had claimed her, and I pressed my lips to the already healing scar on her neck. "That's you, isn't it, baby girl?"

"It is." Tears ran from her face to the sheet below. She reached up with one hand, tracing the lines of my face gently, slowly. "My alpha, I'm yours. I love you."

Chapter 16

Valentine

For the first time in my entire life, since my earliest memories, I wasn't afraid. Donovan Heart was my alpha, and I could feel the bedrock-solid foundation of his love shoring me up with every breath, every step, every thought.

I wasn't alone. I was protected. I was safe.

For four days, we'd made love. He'd done things to my body that I would never have thought I'd like. Every single one of the sex toys had been used, and he'd let me experiment with a few of them on him, too, when I'd asked. He'd kept the plastic knot on almost the whole time, worried he would fall into a rut and hurt me.

But I knew better. We were connected in our souls, and he could feel everything I felt. I wanted to be knotted by him, but I knew better than to press the issue now. We had all the time in the world.

But not really. It was the last week of January, and my heat had more or less broken. We'd video called Dr. Grantham around eight this morning and given her the update. She'd been pleased, but had warned us that it might recur as often as weekly for the first year or two. "Or until you get pregnant," she said, narrowing her eyes with a smile as I covered the claiming bite on my neck. "That could be soon. And after your first pregnancy, your hormones should reset. Then you'll have the normal annual heat cycles like all the other omegas."

We hadn't told her about the knotting issue or brought up fertility. I wasn't sure it would be a problem. Donovan was obsessed with filling me with his cum. Every time he pulled out, he would scoop up the cum that ran out of me, and push it back in, muttering about breeding my pussy. And he wouldn't come in my ass again, or let me swallow. Which kind of sucked. I really did love his flavor.

I needed to remind him whose dick it was, I supposed, throwing my wobbly legs over the side of the well-used nest. I sniffed, picking up more than just sex smells. Something was burning. Toast, maybe.

Naked, I left the nesting room. He'd gone into the kitchen only a few moments before to get some food, but my fingers were itching to cook something a little more complicated. A frittata, maybe. I wandered into the kitchen, and grinned at the picture he made: a Viking wearing only a frilly yellow and white checked apron and socks.

"What are you doing out of your nest, baby?" He had a sad piece of toast in one hand, and was scraping off the burned side into the sink. The eggs on the stove were burning, too, so I quickly slid the pan away from the burner.

"Saving our breakfast, it looks like," I teased. "Let me?"

"You don't have to—" he began, but stopped when I stuck out my lower lip.

"Please, Donovan? You know I love to cook."

"Fuck, that lip," he groaned, leaning down and taking it

softly in between his teeth. "We could just eat each other for breakfast."

"I need food, too. But I will eat my dick later, thank you. And swallow down my dessert." I frowned when he shook his head.

After he put the apron on me—muttering something about dreams coming true—I shooed him away to get dressed, then started pulling out the ingredients to make a real breakfast.

It was the first meal I'd ever been fed by hand, while sitting on a man's lap—though I had a feeling it wouldn't be the last. We had just finished eating when an alarm sounded on Donovan's phone. He stood, his teeth bared. "Go to my bedroom, baby girl."

"W-why? Who's coming?"

"It doesn't matter. The proximity alarm tripped, and you're not dressed for company." I looked down, realizing he was right. All I had on was the frilly apron. I squawked and ran for the bedroom as a car pulled up. The front door opened just as I raced out of sight.

"What the hell are *you* doing here?" Donovan shouted, but he sounded cheerful.

"What part of the contract said to bond the beautiful young client, Mr. Heart?" a voice I knew and loved called out as I yanked a giant Denver Broncos hoodie over my head and looked for some pants. I finally found a pair of long johns I could roll up at my waist and decided that would have to do.

"She's fine. I told Paxson I'd take care of her."

"I'm pretty sure that's not the kind of care he meant."

"Bobby!" I shouted as I ran from the bedroom. I flung myself into Bobby's arms, giving him the biggest hug. We both ignored Donovan's loud growl of displeasure. "How are you back so soon?"

The burly beta man was only a few inches taller than me,

but he lifted his nose and pretended to be looking down. "A hurricane decided to blow through my little patch of Pacific paradise. And then I got a call from my boss, letting me know my favorite omega's bodyguard had quit his job unexpectedly, so I needed to return and make sure she was doing well." He grinned. "Looks like you're doing very well, Val."

I blushed, then went to get him some coffee and a bit of leftover frittata. "I don't think we need a guard, Bobby. No one will come out here. And Donovan has all the tech, like we do at home."

They both ignored me, exchanging those superior nods men liked to give each other. "You'll need to sleep in the cottage out back," Donovan said. "We'll turn the thermostat up, but you might need to grab a few groceries."

"There's a cottage?" I asked, dumbfounded. "Where?"

He grinned. "About a hundred feet from the main house. There's a little pathway with lights."

"How did I not see it? I've been here for days!" I shut up when both men laughed, and Bobby started teasing me about what I'd been spending my time doing.

"Speaking of which," Bobby said, heading for the door, "your sisters sent a few supplies. You texted them that you might need to stay here for a week or two, right?"

I nodded and tried to follow him back outside. Donovan scooped me off the ground, though, and set me on his hip, carrying me outside. Bobby couldn't quite hide his smile as he watched Donovan wrap his long wool coat around me, like I might freeze in a few minutes outside.

He started unpacking the trunk. "They said you'd need something to work on when you weren't... Anyway, they sent you the quilt to finish for Candy and Mr. Paxson, and a present —this little loom and some yarn."

"A saori loom!" I wriggled, trying to get down and see the

boxes. "I've been wanting one for months. You have to order them to be handmade."

"Hold your horses, baby girl," Donovan growled in my ear. My abdomen cramped slightly, and I felt a tiny rush of wet heat between my legs.

"Uh-oh," I whispered, grinding my pelvis into his side.

"Behave," Donovan said with a grunt, as he shifted. His gray sweatpants weren't hiding any part of his erection. I swung the coat over the front of it when Bobby looked up, holding the loom.

"Bring it inside!" I urged.

"And then get out," Donovan muttered.

Laughing, Bobby brought in two suitcases stuffed with my clothes and toiletries that my sisters had packed for me, as well as an enormous bag of yarn and all the pieces of my new Japanese loom. He left it for us to set up, then went to "walk the perimeter" or some such.

Donovan and I were already back in the nest before Bobby had cleared the front porch, getting ready for another wave of heat.

The two weeks after that were the happiest of my life. I video called every member of my family to let them know what was up, though I asked them not to announce it to the press, or even our friends. "It's Nicky and Candy's wedding planning time," I explained when Donovan seemed worried about my reticence.

The days were like an oasis, quiet and filled with beauty. We cooked together, and read side by side. Every day, he went out and chopped firewood for an hour, with no shirt on.

Every day, I watched. Sometimes, I wolf-whistled.

The nonagenarian from the grocery drove her ancient truck up the drive, ostensibly to trade some of her homemade banana bread for some firewood, but really to gather gossip. We didn't mind her knowing about us; the town of Aspen Springs was a sort of family, made up of antisocial, yet deeply generous people. Mating gifts of homemade jams, beef jerky, and even some hothouse vegetables and flowers, showed up at least every other day.

Bobby's boyfriend Glen joined him after the first week, and they became the perfect neighbors, staying close enough to the house that Donovan could relax, but far enough away that they couldn't hear our sex noises.

At least, they acted like they couldn't.

"Is this enough for you, sweetheart?" Donovan asked me one night, as we sat together at a small bonfire behind Bobby and Glen's cottage. "You're so young. Don't you want more nightlife? Dancing or—" I quieted him with a hand over his lips.

"This is the life I never dreamed I could have. A private one. One filled with love, and all the time in the world to make things. I've always been that old lady who knits and bakes, ever since I was a girl. I love not having to pretend I'm a society princess now."

"Do you miss the babies?" he asked after a moment. "Being a sitter?"

I sighed. I had made sure to establish a trust for the center in Denver, and the snuggles with the infants there was the only part of my old life I really missed.

But Donovan snuggled me every morning, and night, and sometimes in between. We had both been at least a little touch starved. We were making up for lost time.

It was one week before my eldest brother's wedding, when the phone rang. It was my sister Kati, letting me know it was time to join the rest of the family and help with the fun and work. I called Bobby to let him know we'd need to start packing, then hung up, snuggled back down on Donovan's lap, and popped his half-hard dick back in my mouth for a few more minutes.

We both enjoyed cock warming, and once he'd understood that it wasn't always about having sex—and that I wasn't trying to sneak some cum into my belly, instead of my vaj—he let me suck on him for as long as I wanted. Right now, he was reading a book on his phone. I was pretty sure it was something about sex, or possibly knots, since he kept getting super hard, then frowning at his dick until it went away.

I gave his dick one last kiss, then sat up, pulling my loose silk robe around my shoulders. I stared at the crackling fire with a sigh. "I don't want to leave." I let my gaze wander around the room, taking in what was no longer an austere space. Now, the corner by the windows was where I kept my loom, with enormous, overflowing baskets of yarn. The quilt I'd finished for Candy and Nicky was folded up at the end of the sofa next to the stacks of books I'd had Bobby bring in. Along the wall were boxes of new pots and pans that we hadn't unpacked, and my sisters had overnighted half my wardrobe. It was a mess.

It looked like a home. My home. And I didn't want to step one foot outside it. Not yet.

"I don't want to share you with anyone."

"Don't you want to see your friends?"

I snorted. "What friends? My sisters are my besties. I'm a homebody, Donovan. Other than my family, you're all I want. And I don't want to share you with anyone."

He looked smug for a moment, then chewed his lip. "You don't regret mating me, do you? You know, you can tell me, if you do. I know I'm not... one of those pretty boys, like your sisters kept bringing around."

Our bond felt shaky for a moment. He really was worried. I

sat up abruptly, tucking his cock back in his briefs. "Is this because I didn't want to make a big announcement? We told your sister and your parents."

He shrugged, but I felt the thread of hurt on our bond. "I want the whole world to know, not just family."

"Donovan, I promise, you're everything I ever dreamed. More than I dared to hope for. I just don't want the press reporting on me, or the family focusing on us instead of Nicky and Candy. We'll have our turn to do all the wedding things..." I blinked furiously, wondering if I'd overstepped. My heart clenched as Donovan just rubbed his forehead, instead of saying anything. "Won't we?"

Instead of answering, he stood and disappeared into his bedroom.

Oh shit. I clutched a hand to my heart, calling myself twelve kinds of idiot for rushing him. Men didn't like to be pressured to get married. And he may have told me he loved me, but he'd never mentioned a wedding. Mating was enough, wasn't it?

Oh god, it would have to be.

"Sweetheart, if you don't stop worrying, I'll have to punish you with orgasms until you can't remember what you were worried about," Donovan said with a smile. He kneeled next to me, shoving a stack of books aside. "Of course I want to marry you. I was hoping to ask you somewhere romantic, though."

He captured my hand in his and drew it to his mouth, kissing it gently. Then he held up a small velvet bag. "I'm not a billionaire," he began. I started to protest, but he tsked. "I said, I'm not a billionaire, but I am a wealthy enough man to buy you a ring of your own. But I thought, maybe..." He opened the pouch, and a gorgeous ring fell into his palm. "My grandmother came over from Iceland when she was a child. This ring was her mother's. Would you wear it, Valentine? Would you wear it, and be my bride—someday?"

I couldn't answer, but I nodded, and he slid the ring onto my finger. It was rose, white, and yellow gold, braided together, with small diamonds hidden in the weave like tiny flowers peeking out from inside the ring.

"Be my wife and live here with me. Have our babies and raise our children. Cook and bake and sew and invite all your family to join us and... be my Valentine forever?"

The bond between us thrummed with hope, and joy, and a love that I knew would last for our whole lives.

"Yes!" I threw myself into his arms. "Oh, Mr. Heart. I'm already yours."

Epilogue

Valentine

Valentine's Day, Four Years Later

"Donovan, time for lunch!" I called from the porch, peering around the side of our house. The day was more than chilly, and I pulled the fuzzy blanket-coat he'd given me that morning closer around my shoulders. I sucked in a deep breath, loving the fresh pine and snow scent of winter, as always.

My husband had bundled both our children into a wagon and trundled them down the shoveled path to the cabin where Bobby lived with his husband for half the year.

Bobby had retired from bodyguarding to be the godfather of our three-year-old twin boys, and our betasitter whenever he and Glen weren't at their other home on the Big Island. He'd been hinting broadly that they could betasit for three just as easily as two, and might even be willing to stay here full-time if they were needed. I'd laughed it off, but Donovan had gotten a gleam in his eye.

Everyone was surprised we only had two children, with

119

being bonded true mates. Of course, we hadn't shared the particulars of our sex life with anyone—except for my sisters, of course.

Donovan was still terrified of hurting me. But he'd been seeing a therapist for a while now, one who specialized in PTSD. He'd struggled with the diagnosis, but had thrown himself into trying to heal. Watching me give birth to our twins and seeing their enormous noggins emerge from my vagina had gone a long way to helping him understand the flexibility of a woman's body. But my omega had been unsatisfied during my last annual heat, and that was what finally made him agree to make a real attempt.

He wanted to give me what my omega needed, what I needed to be happy. And apparently, that was a quadruple-decker cheeseburger. Well, veggie burger.

I hoped he was ready now, because just thinking of that knot had my inner omega doing warm-up stretches, and sending slick to get things ready downstairs.

I heard Donovan whistling as he jogged back to the house, and I raced inside, heading straight to the nest. Of course, we'd had to build onto the main house after the boys arrived. But we'd left the original windowless bedroom alone. We had far too many wonderful memories of that little space.

By the time he walked in, the lights were dimmed, the blankets were all in place, and the room smelled like warm cinnamon custard.

"Sweetheart?" Donovan stopped stock-still in the doorway, taking in my pale pink lingerie set. "It's time? I thought we had a few hours."

"I got too excited," I admitted as he began to strip off his clothing. He was forty-three, and his temples now had salt mixed with the pepper, but his daily wood-chopping and mountain runs kept him looking as much like a Viking as ever.

"What got you so worked up, baby girl?" he murmured, grabbing the silicone ring from the shelf of toys. He stopped at the edge of my nest, about to slip it over his rigid cock. "May I enter your nest, Omega?"

I met his eyes. "Yes, but not with that on." I chewed at my lip, hoping he would understand.

He kneeled and took a deep breath, calming himself. "I can do this," he said after a moment. "I might need your help. But I can do this."

"I know you can. You can do anything."

We went slowly, kissing and stroking, until my heat spiked. We both had sweat dampening our hair, and he'd wrung three orgasms from me, but I was still in control enough to help him overcome his fear.

"Lie down, my love," I whispered, and he obeyed, though his brow was faintly creased with worry. I swung my leg over him like I was mounting a horse. "Yeehaw." I grinned, making him laugh. I slid his cock all around my soaked entrance, loving the satiny feel of him, and then slowly, *slowly* took him inside. "Remember, keep your hips still. Let me do the work this time, okay?"

He nodded mutely, his breath sawing in and out as I thrust over him. I loved the stretch of his cock, and I rode him until he gasped, "Please."

Donovan loved to be in control in the bedroom, and letting me take charge might have been as hard as knowing what we were about to try. I changed the angle slightly, so that the tip of his cock hit my favorite spot.

"Tell me to come, Daddy," I moaned. "I need to come."

"Not yet, baby," he said, grunting as the first part of his knot slid inside. He tucked his hands behind his back, closing his eyes as I descended again, and a little more of the swollen knot slipped in. I was so slick, it was actually hard not to just slam down over him.

But every movement had to be felt. Smooth. Intentional. I whispered how good it felt, hoping he could hear the truth in my words. Knowing he had to feel it in our bond.

The walls of my pussy were beginning to flutter, the climax taking over. Only years of letting Donovan control my orgasms held me back from the edge now.

"Now." His word echoed my thoughts, and I slid down, encasing the entire length of him inside, just as my climax barreled over me. We locked eyes, and I smiled as I felt him begin to come. His gaze was filled with equal parts lust and concern, but when the knot filled me, it triggered something I'd never felt.

It was as if my climaxes were a waterfall of pleasure, and I was being carried over without any control. I cried out, hoping the bond was helping him to feel what I felt. To know some small part of this joy.

Donovan's cries joined mine as he filled me, wet heat jetting up into my swollen channel, mixing with my slick, trapped by the knot.

"It feels so... fucking... *good*," I mumbled a few lifetimes later, once I could speak again.

Donovan laughed. "Is that your way of saying you want a punishment?"

I giggled, the movement making his knot swell the tiniest bit more. "It's my way of saying I want all of my dick, inside me, for the next week." I winked. "I guess you can punish me at the same time, if you like."

He let out an exaggerated sigh. "You're not afraid of me in the least, are you?"

"Not even a little, Alpha."

With a heart as big as his, and a quadruple-sized knot to top it off? There was no room inside me for anything but love.

Thank you so much for reading! I hope you loved getting to know Valentine and Donovan. If you have time to leave a rating or review, it would make *my* heart sing. Rainbow's Storm is next!

Acknowledgments

Thank you to my sister who helped me make a list over the holidays and check it twice. Donovan Heart wouldn't be the same without you! (But why didn't we think about Mom reading this? #noragrets)

Roses and chocolates to my editor Raewyn Ash, my PA Darcy Bennett, and my cover designer Kate Farlow for making me look polished, when we all know I'm a creatively disorganized mess.

My deepest thanks got to the Perfect Pink Posse members who jumped in to help smooth this one out so quickly. Courtney, Bekka, Jacquie, Kristin, Maria, Renee, and Megan are the sweethearts I don't deserve. But I'll keep trying to show you how much you mean to me!

Finally, thank *you*, Dear Reader, for sharing in the fun of these filthy, fluffy books. Every time you leave a review, or send an email or message letting me know how much you enjoyed one of my stories, you make my day so much brighter. If you keep reading? I'll keep writing.

Also by Merri Bright

The Billionaire's Betasitter Series (MF Omegaverse)

Knotty New Year

Sunshine's Grump

Grumpy's Holiday Sweater

Rainbow's Storm

The Forgotten Angel Series (Why Choose Paranormal)

Lost Feather

Fallen Feather

Rising Feather

Glittering Feather

The Lost Lines Series (Why Choose Fantasy)

Vali's Stories:

The Omega's Mischief: A Short Story Prequel

The King's Omega: The Lost Lines Series Book 1

The Queen's Nest: A Lost Lines Series Novella

Haven's Story:

The Guards' Haven

Cilla's Story:

The Duchess's Designs

Roya's Story:

The Assassin's Promise

Wren's Story:

Part One The Leviathan's Debt

Part Two The Wyvern's Redemption

About the Author

Merri Bright spends her days dreaming up naughty angels, misunderstood demons, sexy shifters, growly Alpha males, and frequently refuses to limit her heroines to just one love interest.

Please join Merri's Mischief Makers on Facebook where you'll discover random giveaways, sneak peeks of new novels, book recommendations, and silly/sexy/funny stuff. You can also email her at merri@merribright.com, or follow/subscribe to reamstories.com/merribright for stories in progress.